Patrick's
Notebook

Words
of Love
from

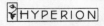

New York

Patrick's Notebook

by Patrick Thornhart

COPYRIGHT © 1996, ABC/DAYTIME PRESS

Photo on page iii © E. J. Carr

Designed by Holly McNeely

ISBN 0-7868-8226-3

FIRST EDITION

10   9   8   7   6   5   4   3   2   1

for Margaret

Love.

It can make you feel the greatest joy and the deepest pain. It can bring a smile to your face and tears to your eyes. Love leads you on a journey of discovery, to places you never imagined. It can possess you and make you powerless to deny its existence. Touched by love, your life will change forever.

When Margaret Saybrooke entered my life, my world as I knew it ceased to exist. How could I ever have known that I would fall in love so deeply, so painfully, with the one woman who could make me feel free and alive. From the first moment we kissed, my heart and soul belonged to her, and hers to me. And yet, I sit here with my heart nearly breaking with love and with an emptiness in my soul since the fates have chosen to keep us apart.

Poets and wordsmiths through the ages have told the tale of the power of love shared, the joy of its passion and the pain of yearning when true love is denied. When I think of Margaret and the force of my feelings causes my words to fall short, I look to these words of love to express what I feel inside.

Patrick's
Notebook

All my life I've scoffed at the age-old platitude that "being born Irish means that someday the world will break your heart." No longer do I mock the notion, for here I sit—*a heartbroken Irishman*—trying to make some sense out of my maelstrom of a life. Where to begin? Perhaps at the beginning, on that chilly autumn night, barely a year ago, when I took shelter in the Wild Swan Inn on the Irish isle of Inishcrag—and set my eyes upon an earthbound angel. Only later would I learn her name, Margaret Saybrooke.

Margaret "Marty" Saybrooke could think of nothing more pleasurable than unwinding in this quaint Irish pub, sipping a cup of tea, and reflecting on the events of this, one of the most immensely satisfying days of her young life. Barely in her twenties, Margaret Saybrooke had already endured more personal loss than most people do in a lifetime.

As a child Margaret lost the two people she loved most in the world when her parents drowned. After their untimely death, she was left in the care of her careless Aunt Kiki, a flighty and irresponsible socialite who exercised little parental control over her impres-

I shall write and write here of our love, so it will never die.

One Day I Wrote Her Name
Edmund Spenser

One day I wrote her name upon the strand,
But came the waves and washèd it away:
Again I wrote it with a second hand,
But came the tide and made my pains his prey.
"Vain man," said she, "that dost in vain essay
A mortal thing so to immortalize;
For I myself shall like to this decay,
And eke my name be wipèd out likewise."
"Not so," quoth I; "let baser things devise
To die in dust, but you shall live by fame;
My verse your virtues rare shall eternize,
And in the heavens write your glorious name:
Where, whenas Death shall all the world subdue,
Our love shall live, and later life renew."

sionable niece—while doing her best to deplete the girl's trust fund.

I would later learn that Margaret had journeyed to the remote isle of Inishcrag, not for pleasure, but to conquer a lifelong fear—by standing up to Aunt Kiki! For months, Kiki Saybrooke had been squandering Margaret's inheritance in a wild spending spree throughout Europe. On this triumphant day, Margaret successfully confronted the loveless woman who raised her, and cut her off!

The smell of smoldering peat filled the room on this clear and windy Irish night. Outside, a full moon brightened the October night, prompting the barkeep, wise old Tommy Kenneally, to share an old legend with the pretty young visitor from the States. "The isle of Inishcrag is enchanted, you know. Who so kisses a newcomer on Inishcrag beneath the full moon on this island—that man becomes yours forever."

As she reflected on the day's achievements, Margaret didn't notice me finishing my glass of Irish whiskey and starting out the door. Just then I froze in my tracks, a look of panic in my eyes. Two burly men had walked in the pub,

You've suffered terribly in life and it is that sorrow deep within your soul that compels me most.

Sonnet, to Geneva
   Lord Byron

Thine eye's blue tenderness, thy long fair hair,
And the wan lustre of thy features—caught
From contemplation—where serenely wrought,
Seems Sorrow's softness charm'd from its despair—
Have thrown such speaking sadness in thine air,
That—but I know thy blessed bosom fraught
With mines of unalloy'd and stainless thought—
I should have deem'd thee doom'd to earthly care.

and I knew instantly that they were looking for me.

I quickly turned, my eyes rapidly scanning the room. They came to rest on the girl with the long, flowing locks, contentedly sitting in the snuggery by the fire.

"Darling, there you are," I said, sidling up beside Margaret. And before she could utter a word of reply, I kissed her passionately! Breathlessly, Margaret broke from the kiss with an incredulous smile that quickly turned to fear as the impact of the moment set in.

"Let me go!" she exclaimed.

"Please, miss," I whispered with a pleading sense of urgency in my voice. "It's a matter of life and death. We've got to pretend we are lovers."

Without a second to ponder what was happening, she played along, engaging me—a man she'd never met—in seemingly intimate conversation. The two thugs searched the pub, but not seeing their prey, they took off into the night. I breathed a hefty sigh of relief, and thanked my "wife" for taking part in this hastily arranged charade. By acting casually and posing as my wife, she had helped me elude my hunters. This precious angel had saved my life!

"Darling, there you are," I said, sidling up beside the wonderously enchanting woman in the Wild Swan Inn. My sudden appearance surely startled her, but before she could utter a word of reply, I kissed her passionately!

"That was close," I uttered gratefully. "I always thought angels had halos."

Safe—for the moment—I hurried out the door. Glancing back, I took one last look at my sweet savior. She sat transfixed, seemingly overcome with an uncanny sense of wonderment and fear, attraction, and apprehension. How she must have puzzled over what had just transpired.

Later I would learn so much more about this lovely lass. For one, she had a boyfriend back in the States—although they had recently had (as you Yanks are wont to say) a "major falling out." His name was Dylan Moody, and he had been the prime source of strength and stability throughout Margaret's sojourn toward self-esteem. When her parents died, Margaret lost any sense of emotional security, and callous Aunt Kiki had made certain it was never restored. As a child, she began acting out. As a teenager, she earned her reputation as Llanview's poor little rich girl, a hellion who spread scandalous gossip, went on wild drinking binges, and turned the town of Llanview upside down.

I would learn much later that Margaret's

*Fate makes us waste our
precious time . . .
oh, what a shame.*

O Mistress Mine
William Shakespeare

O mistress mine, where are you roaming?
O! stay and hear; your true love's coming,
   That can sing both high and low.
Trip no further, pretty sweeting;
Journeys end in lovers meeting,
   Every wise man's son doth know.

What is love? 'Tis not hereafter;
Present mirth hath present laughter;
   What's to come is still unsure.
In delay there lies no plenty;
Then, come kiss me, sweet and twenty;
   Youth's a stuff will not endure.

path to self-destruction eventually led her, one fateful night, to the Kappa Alpha Delta fraternity house at Llanview University, where she was brutally gang-raped. That horrible incident was the low point in her sorry and sorrowful life, taking away any feeling of personal security and self-sufficiency that she'd been able to achieve. The road to self-discovery had been slow, but rewarding. In the fall of 1995, Margaret Saybrooke was no longer the village pariah. She had taken control of her life—and how wonderful it must have felt to be so . . . so . . . *free!*

Retiring to her bedroom at the Wild Swan Inn, Margaret suddenly heard a strange sound. Whirling around, she was stunned to see me climbing through her window! Once again, I begged for her assistance. No doubt my daring entrance had shaken her up, yet I could feel that she trusted me in some innate sort of way. She agreed to hide me from the two men who were hot on my trail. Our second moment together was equally as fleeting as the earlier encounter in the pub. The danger passed. With the coast finally clear, I prepared to depart yet again.

"It was a wonderful marriage while it

I've often wondered, Margaret, what you were like as a small child— despite all the harm that the world has done to you, your radiant, childlike beauty still shines through.

There Is a Garden in Her Face
Thomas Campion

There is a garden in her face,
   Where roses and white lilies grow,
A heavenly paradise is that place,
   Wherein all pleasant fruits do flow.
There cherries grow, which none may buy,
Till "Cherry ripe" themselves do cry.

Those cherries fairly do enclose
   Of orient pearl a double row,
Which when her lovely laughter shows,
   They look like rosebuds filled with snow.
Yet them nor peer nor prince can buy,
Till "Cherry ripe" themselves do cry.

Her eyes like angels watch them still;
   Her brows like bended bows do stand,
Threatening with piercing frowns to kill
   All that attempt with eye or hand
Those sacred cherries to come nigh
Till "Cherry ripe" themselves do cry.

lasted," I quipped, taking her head in my hands and kissing her lips lightly.

"So long, angel," I whispered, before climbing through the window and disappearing into the moonlit night. Though danger lurked in my path, I was stirred by this unmistakably sensual exchange, and I now feel certain that she felt the passion with equal ardor. Margaret told me later how she stared out into the dark night wondering, "Who was this Irishman who kissed me under a full moon?"

I'm sure that my midnight antics left her puzzled, but the pieces would begin to fall into place the following day when I returned yet again. This time, my angel wanted answers.

"What's really going on?" she demanded. Thinking fast, I spun a tale, informing her that my name was Michael O'Neill, a physicist doing highly confidential work for the Irish government. The men who were chasing me? They were merely local police who had mistaken me for a burglar. I breathed a tiny sigh of relief. Margaret, however, remained skeptical.

"How do I know you are telling the truth?" she queried.

"In your whole life, have you ever seen a face as honest as this?" I quickly replied with

*How brief our carefree moments
on Inishcrag were and yet . . . .
they were a lifetime.*

Mother Ocean
Thorsten Kaye

She walks along my country's shore
Behind her lonely guard
And holds in every step she takes
The rhythm of my heart

Oh broken cliffs of Ireland
Lay down as soft white sand
And guide her on a steady path
When I can't be at hand

And raging winds that shaped these hills
Caress her face with care
Forgive the sadness in her eyes
And gently stroke her hair

Now mother ocean lift her high
If she must leave by sea
Take her safely where she must
Then bring her home to me . . .

just a hint of a smile on my fatigued face. With my back against the wall, I clearly demonstrated to Ms. Saybrooke the Irish gift of bright-hearted charm. She would soon discover that I also had the Irish curse of romantic melancholy.

When I dozed off in her room, Margaret surreptitiously searched the pockets of my jacket. A quick glimpse at my passport proved to Margaret that I was not as honest as I'd claimed. The document revealed my real name: Patrick Thornhart! From another pocket she pulled a folded piece of sheet music—spattered with blood! Before she could react further, I awakened and grabbed for her hand, demanding to know what she was doing. Clearly, I needed to provide her with some straight answers. Yes, I admitted that my name was Patrick Thornhart, but I still chose to insist that I was a physicist on a government mission.

Patrick Thornhart was indeed my name, but a physicist? Hardly! I'm actually a writer by profession and a poet by nature. Raised in County Kildare to a poor, large, affectionate family, I grew up with a love of my country, of its poetry and its beauty. To earn a living, I teach school, having recently earned a post at

We may have nothing now . . . I hope in time we'll have it all.

Grow Old Along with Me
    Robert Browning

    Grow old along with me!
The best is yet to be,
The last of life, for which the first was made,
Our times are in his hand
Who saith, "A whole I planned,
Youth shows but half; trust God: see all, nor be afraid!"

Without your beauty,
I will surely die.

A Thing of Beauty (from *Endymion*)
John Keats

A thing of beauty is a joy for ever;
Its loveliness increases; it will never
Pass into nothingness; but still will keep
A bower quiet for us, and a sleep
Full of sweet dreams, and health, and quiet breathing.
Therefore, on every morrow, are we wreathing
A flowery band to bind us to the earth,
Spite of despondence, of the inhuman dearth
Of noble natures, of the gloomy days,
Of all the unhealthy and o'er-darkened ways
Made for our searching: yes, in spite of all,
Some shape of beauty moves away the pall
From our dark spirits. Such the sun, the moon,
Trees old and young, sprouting a shady boon
For simple sheep; and such are daffodils
With the green world they live in; and clear rills

That for themselves a cooling covert make
'Gainst the hot season; the mid-forest brake,
Rich with a sprinkling of fair musk-rose blooms:
And such too is the grandeur of the dooms
We have imagined for the mighty dead;
All lovely tales that we have heard or read:
An endless fountain of immortal drink,
Pouring unto us from the heaven's brink.
Nor do we merely feel these essences
For one short hour; no, even as the trees
That whisper round a temple become soon
Dear as the temple's self, so does the moon,
The passion poesy, glories infinite,
Haunt us till they become a cheering light
Unto our souls, and bond to us so fast,
That, whether there be shine, or gloom o'ercast,
They always must be with us, or we die.

Trinity College in Dublin, where, if I must say so, my gift of gab, passion for my work, and (some might say) handsome countenance made me a very popular young professor. I loved Dublin, the bustle of the city, the nightlife of the young, the brightest, the wildest. Now, on the run on the tranquil isle of Inishcrag, I kept my true identity a closely guarded secret from the young American woman who had already changed my life forever.

"Thank you for being my angel, I'll never forget it. Now, just let me slip out of your life. I'll ask no more of you."

Margaret knew I was lying, yet, strangely, she could not let go. Searching my troubled face, she saw something in it she trusted. It had never been easy for Margaret Saybrooke to trust anyone.

Margaret wavered. She stopped me in my tracks, asking about the music.

"Would you play it for me?" I asked.

"Yes. Oh, and by the way, my name is Marty Saybrooke."

I looked on in awe as "Marty" finished playing the hauntingly beautiful yet incomplete tune on the piano in the Wild Swan Inn. As she finished, this lovely, soulful lass lifted

It gave me unparalleled joy to hear Margaret playing such beautiful music on the piano at the Wild Swan. She told me it made her feel free — and it had been a long time since she'd felt that way.

19

her eyes from the keys and stared into this Irishman's eyes. For a fleeting moment, time stopped, only to be resumed by the piercing call of a ferry whistle echoing through the inn. Preparing to leave in time to catch the last boat off the island, I bid her farewell.

"You're a beautiful lady. That's obvious. You're talented and smart, it's just as clear. But even something else—you've got bravery. A man would be lucky to have you standing by his side, Margaret Saybrooke."

I leaned over to kiss her hand, and suddenly felt the barrel of a gun in my back. A second man appeared. "Don't make a sound. Very quietly, come with us and walk out to the car."

Terrified, we were shuttled off to an abandoned Celtic church, where we learned that our captor was Chief Inspector Quilligan of the Irish Special Branch. "We're kind of like your CIA," he smiled to Margaret before ushering her out of earshot so he could have a private talk with me, his intended prey. Once Margaret was sequestered, Quilligan demanded the sheet music, which I explained had been given to me by my fiancée, Siobhan Connelly, soon after she was shot in Belfast. I explained to him that, with her dying breath, Siobhan

Miles from Home
Thorsten Kaye

Miles from home
Country roads might still remember
All the times I kicked along
My head pulled down by sorrow
With another first love gone
And when the night fell without warning
I grew up without a sound
Our dreams scratched into table tops
Across this Irish town . . .

There were old trees by the water
Restless waves played with their leaves
My heart reached out to all the world
Had never heard the word naïve
And when the day broke I was dreaming
Of how to leave these haunted plains
And all the death or glory boys
Carried by the wind

I disregard the old reminders
Every time they dance my way
And in my soul I light a candle
For all the words I didn't say
When the night falls without warning
Another day will leave me torn
With my heart back where it's always been
And my body miles from home
My body miles from home . . .

I had no idea who was after me or what the danger was that hounded me, but I knew I couldn't put your life in danger. I would have to let you go.

"You're a beautiful lady. That's obvious. You're talented and smart, it's just as clear. But even something else — you've got bravery. A man would be lucky to have you standing by his side, Margaret Saybrooke."

(who, I was staggered to learn, was a field agent for the Special Branch) pleaded with me to go to Inishcrag and give the music to Quilligan. On this stormy night, I at last fulfilled the promise made to my fiancée before she died in my arms. I handed over the bloody sheet of music to Quilligan.

"Siobhan's murder will not go unpunished," he promised.

"And what about Miss Saybrooke?"

For one brief moment
on a deserted island
I felt myself
born anew.

A Birthday
Christina Rossetti

My heart is like a singing bird
    Whose nest is in a watered shoot;
My heart is like an apple-tree
    Whose boughs are bent with thick-set fruit;
My heart is like a rainbow shell
    That paddles in a halcyon sea;
My heart is gladder than all these,
    Because my love is come to me.

Raise me a dais of silk and down;
    Hang it with vair and purple dyes;
Carve it in doves and pomegranates,
    And peacocks with a hundred eyes;
Work it in gold and silver grapes,
    In leaves and silver fleurs-de-lys;
Because the birthday of my life
    Is come, my love is come to me.

"Stick to your story—you're a physicist. Top secret," answered Quilligan. I felt uneasy about perpetuating this lie, but knew it was for the best—this innocent American girl must be kept out of my Irish peril.

Before setting me free, Quilligan issued a word of caution, warning me to steer clear of anyone wearing or carrying a coin bearing the insignia "21." If I should encounter anyone with such an object, I was instructed to contact Quilligan, or his superior, Bass, in Dublin.

It is clear to me now that Quilligan was not sharing his true motive with me in the ruins of that Celtic church. Later, I was chilled to discover that I was being used as bait to smoke out the opposition group, "Men of 21." They desperately wanted to get their hands on that sheet music. And they knew, or thought they knew, that I had it! I can only imagine the conversation that Quilligan must have had with his cohort, Mr. McCann, when Margaret and I were out of earshot.

"So, Thornhart, poor man, will lead us to the Men of 21," he must have boasted. "Let's hope he stays alive long enough to do it."

Margaret and I returned, safe and sound, to the Wild Swan, but, more than ever, I could

As I see you Margaret,
in my eyes.

First Love
John Clare

I ne'er was struck before that hour
    With love so sudden and so sweet,
Her face it bloomed like a sweet flower
    And stole my heart away complete.
My face turned pale as deadly pale,
    My legs refused to walk away,
And when she looked, what could I ail?
    My life and all seemed turned to clay.

And then my blood rushed to my face
    And took my eyesight quite away,
The trees and bushes round the place
    Seemed midnight at noonday.
I could not see a single thing,
    Words from my eyes did start—
They spoke as chords do from the string,
    And blood burnt round my heart.

Are flowers the winter's choice?
    Is love's bed always snow?
She seemed to hear my silent voice,
    Not love's appeals to know.
I never saw so sweet a face
    As that I stood before.
My heart has left its dwelling-place
    And can return no more.

feel deep peril permeating the air. Sensing that I was, in some way, being used, I knew I must do everything in my power to keep my angel Margaret safe from harm. With mixed feelings, I stood by as she checked out of the inn and prepared to leave for home. But Margaret wasn't going anywhere. A violent storm had forced the cancellation of all ferries to the mainland—and now there was no room at the inn!

I spoke up.

"Where are my manners?" I politely asked, holding back a laugh. "You're welcome to stay . . . in my room . . . *Miss* Saybrooke."

Once again, fate and the elements had thrown us together. Weary from the day's escapades, I began to strip off my shirt. Catching sight of my near nakedness, she gasped!

"Whoa! Hey! Why don't you go down the hall and use the bathroom to change into your pajamas!" she exclaimed.

"I don't wear pajamas. I've slept in nothing but the skin God gave me since I was a lad."

To our mutual amusement, we spent the night in single beds, separated by a blanket thrown over a clothesline. Before shutting my

Our first night together in the same room echoed the old Celtic
legend of Tristan and Isolde. The star-crossed lovers placed a
naked sword between them when they lay on the same bed. As in
a scene out of an old movie, Margaret preferred placing a
blanket over a rope to keep us apart.

eyes for a fitful night of sleep, I offered my guest a bit of verse:

"*Good night my little chickapea of a wife/Sure if the seas are willin',/and the rain stops fallin',I'll be off to Dublin in the mornin'.*"

"Are all the Thornharts as crazy as you?" chuckled Margaret.

"I suppose we're all a bit daft, but I think I've mastered the art of it."

For several days a howling storm pounded the isle of Inishcrag. Ferries remained canceled, giving Margaret and me precious moments to share heart-to-heart talks in front of a roaring fire at the Wild Swan. When the stormy weather abated a bit, we ventured out into the countryside, sharing bicycle rides and long walks through the rolling hills. I felt a strong but unspoken attraction. Did she?

As I see you Margaret, in my eyes.

One night, a near-tragedy brought us even closer. Margaret (who I would learn had an intense fear of water ever since her parents drowned when she was a very young girl) panicked when we were asked to help out in a crisis—there had been a terrible boating wreck at sea and the victims needed assistance. Without hesitation, I headed out into the storm, but

Stanzas for Music
   Lord Byron

There be none of Beauty's daughters
With a magic like thee;
And like music on the waters
Is thy sweet voice to me:
When, as if its sound were causing
The charm'd ocean's pausing,
The waves lie still and gleaming,
And the lull'd winds seem dreaming.

And the midnight moon is weaving
Her bright chain o'er the deep;
Whose breast is gently heaving,
As an infant's sleep:
So the spirit bows before thee,
To listen and adore thee;
With a full but soft emotion,
Like the swell of Summer's ocean.

Perfect Woman
    William Wordsworth

She was a phantom of delight
When first she gleam'd upon my sight;
A lovely apparition, sent
To be a moment's ornament;
Her eyes as stars of twilight fair;
Like twilight's, too, her dusky hair;
But all things else about her drawn
From May-time and the cheerful dawn;
A dancing shape, an image gay,
To haunt, to startle, and waylay.

I saw her upon nearer view,
A Spirit, yet a Woman too!
Her household motions light and free,
And steps of virgin liberty;
A countenance in which did meet
Sweet records, promises as sweet;
A creature not too bright or good
For human nature's daily food;
For transient sorrows, simple wiles,
Praise, blame, love, kisses, tears, and smiles.

And now I see with eye serene
The very pulse of the machine;
A being breathing thoughtful breath,
A traveller between life and death;
The reason firm, the temperate will,
Endurance, foresight, strength, and skill;
A perfect Woman, nobly plann'd,
To warn, to comfort, and command;
And yet a Spirit still, and bright
With something of angelic light.

Margaret stood frozen with fear, unable to move.

"Margaret, you're a medical student! You've got to help this woman! Margaret, listen to me!" I urged.

"No, she drowned. She drowned."

"No. No. No, Margaret. You couldn't help your parents, but it may be that you can help this woman!" She stood immobile, paralyzed by the horrible memory from her past. I implored her to act.

"Margaret Saybrooke, look at me! I know you can do this. I know how strong you are. I've seen it. I'm counting on you one more time!"

Margaret overcame her fear and joined with me to assist the villagers in saving countless lives. Wet and shivering, Margaret and I staggered back to our cozy room, clinging to each other. It had been a night of heroics. A night of overcoming lifelong fears. And it was to be a night of revelation.

For the first time, Margaret opened up, telling me about Dylan Moody, the young man she "cared about a lot" who had defied her and opened a community center in the most dangerous section of Llanview. The fact that Dylan was trying to rid the area of gang violence

Margaret's lifelong fear of drowning was put to the test when she came to the aid of the unfortunate victims of a boating disaster. When the crisis passed, I proudly wrapped my arms around her, assuring Margaret that she was just as strong as I knew she could be.

unnerved Marty Saybrooke. He was taking his life in his hands, and Margaret told me that she could not bear the thought of losing him. A violent sea had taken the lives of her parents. Now she was afraid to lose the man she loved to an act of senseless inner-city violence. The friction had proven too much, Margaret explained, and she had broken off her relationship with Dylan.

"I understand," I responded, with a painful quiver in my usually powerful voice. It was my turn to share my most intimate thoughts. We drew even closer as I shared the still raw tale of my fiancée's violent death, carefully leaving out the details of her involvement with the Irish Secret Branch. Privately, the truth about Siobhan's secret life continued to stagger me. How could I have known her so well, and not at all? Siobhan was dead, and now I was determined to keep Margaret Saybrooke, who had innocently stumbled upon these grim and dangerous circumstances, from suffering a similar fate.

"Ireland is a very violent country. Beautiful but violent. But tonight we are safe." As Marty drifted off to sleep, I lay beside her in the half dark, stroking her hair.

Stanzas for Music
     Lord Byron

You and the sea, Margaret, are forever linked in my mind.

They say that Hope is happiness;
But genuine Love must prize the past,
And Memory wakes the thoughts that bless;
They rose the first—they set the last;

And all that Memory loves the most
Was once our only Hope to be,
And all that Hope adored and lost
Hath melted into Memory.

Alas! it is delusion all:
The future cheats us from afar,
Nor can we be what we recall,
Nor dare we think on what we are.

35

Later that evening, I met privately with Chief Inspector Quilligan who confirmed what I had suspected—I and my precious piece of sheet music (which I'd already turned over to the Special Branch) were being used as bait to smoke out the "Men of 21," an international terrorist group. I was reluctant at first, but Quilligan persuaded me to join his efforts and thus avenge my fiancée's death. I agreed, but with one stipulation: that Quilligan promise to get the American girl out of Ireland to safety.

Margaret could not get the image of the bloodied sheet music out of her head as she prepared to leave Inishcrag—and me—forever. The tune was haunting, strangely melodic— what could it really mean? And was it more . . . more than just music? After hastily packing her bags, she was in no mood to engage in small talk as we sat in the snuggery at the Wild Swan Inn. She had overheard a bit of my conversation with Quilligan. Now she pressed for answers.

"Why don't you tell me what Quilligan meant by using you to smoke out the "Men of 21"? You're still in danger, aren't you?" I couldn't help but reel from her hard-hitting questions. She was obviously getting close to

After death, remember me as I truly am.

Song
    Christina Rossetti

When I am dead, my dearest,
    Sing no sad songs for me;
Plant thou no roses at my head,
    Nor shady cypress tree:
Be the green grass above me
    With showers and dewdrops wet;
And if thou wilt, remember,
    And if thou wilt, forget.

I shall not see the shadows,
    I shall not feel the rain;
I shall not hear the nightingale
    Sing on, as if in pain;
And dreaming through the twilight
    That doth not rise nor set,
Haply I may remember,
    And haply may forget.

the truth. Upon my confessing that I wasn't going back to Dublin, it suddenly hit her. She realized that I was planning to sacrifice my life for the cause!

It was chillingly true. By allowing myself to be used as bait to smoke out the mysterious "Men of 21," I was issuing my own death sentence. Margaret strongly suspected that the sheet music was somehow involved. And she knew in her heart that I was pushing her away, shielding her from . . . *something!*

Our intense conversation was broken by the arrival of Mr. Kenneally, the barkeep, who invited us to join in an Irish jig in the center of the inn. I recall that Margaret resisted, insisting that we had to finish our talk. I, on the other hand, was more than willing to use this pleasant diversion to avoid further discussion. On the dance floor, I cajoled Margaret, teaching her a few steps of the hearty dance I'd learned as a child in knee pants. Our hands touched, our bodies brushed, our eyes met as we took center stage and danced a bright and happy jig for all to see. As the guests applauded our dancing exploits, Mr. Kenneally made a jovial announcement:

*Love and passion
are but one.*

A White Rose
John Boyle O'Reilly

The red rose whispers of passion,
　And the white rose breathes of love;
O, the red rose is a falcon,
　And the white rose is a dove.

But I send you a cream-white rosebud
　With a flush upon its petal tips;
For the love that is purest and sweetest
　Has a kiss of desire on the lips.

"That's what happens when you kiss under a full moon. You fall in love!"

That moment of joy was spellbinding—but acutely brief.

"Go back to America. Go back to your life and stay the hell away from me!" I bellowed as Margaret once again pressed for the truth. Stung by my harsh words, she ran from the inn in tears. I sat, alone and distressed, knowing in my heart how much I cared for her. Still, I simply couldn't let someone I cared for be in danger again. It would be better—and safer—if Margaret simply went home.

She came back to the inn, this time with her bags in tow. Stalwartly, she moved toward me and thrust out her hand.

"Goodbye, good luck," she coldly stated, holding back any emotion.

"Believe me, it's better this way, Margaret" I countered, grabbing her and kissing her. I'll not soon forget that moment—it was a full, fervent, impassioned kiss that left my angel breathless. But the moment could not linger. So I pushed Margaret away, gruffly imploring her to "get on the ferry and get as far away from me as she could." With the ferry bell clanging in the distance, I watched as a forlorn Margaret

Margaret and I could always count on our twinkly-eyed innkeeper, Tommy Kenneally, to provide us with a bit of wise counsel, or to weave us an ancient Celtic legend. But in time, even Kenneally came to believe that I was a cold hearted, cold-blooded killer!

joined the others heading for the boat. In utter despair, I sank into my chair and dropped my head into my hands. Margaret was gone. Forever. Or was she? Within a moment, the door of the inn flew open and there she was! Seeing my despondent nature must have touched something inside her. She slipped in beside me.

"Please, it's a matter of life and death. We've got to pretend we are lovers," declared Margaret, and proceeded to kiss me—just as I had done on that fateful night of their first meeting! My angel explained that she had returned because she knew in her heart that there was something strong and true between us, and she couldn't leave forever without knowing what it was.

"How am I supposed to sail away into the night knowing I'd never see you again? And what did you think I'd do when you kissed me like that and told me to go away, just disappear meekly? You see, you've picked the wrong wife, Patrick!"

Facing such a feisty soul, I had no choice but to tell Margaret what she needed to hear. How could I deny this woman with the angelic visage—and deeply suspicious nature? I pro-

Love expressed can never touch the love that's really in our hearts.

Sonnet 23
William Shakespeare

As an unperfect actor on the stage,
Who with his fear is put besides his part,
Or some fierce thing replete with too much rage,
Whose strength's abundance weakens his own heart;
So I, for fear of trust, forget to say
The perfect ceremony of love's rite,
And in mine own love's strength seem to decay,
O'ercharged with burden of mine own love's might.
O, let my books be then the eloquence
And dumb presagers of my speaking breast,
Who plead for love and look for recompense
More than that tongue that more hath more expressed.
O, learn to read what silent love hath writ;
To hear with eyes belongs to love's fine wit.

ceeded to confide in Margaret, telling her the whole truth, starting with my real identity.

"I *am* Patrick Thornhart, but while I think that the second law of thermodynamics has to do with heat and motion or something like that, I can't swear to it because I'm not a physicist. I was no doubt reading Yeats when they were trying to teach me physics!"

At first, the words came quietly, with great difficultly. Soon, I opened up about everything . . . Siobhan, Quilligan, the Men of 21, the "bait." We moved upstairs where the words poured out of me. Margaret listened in amazement as I detailed the whole sorrowful tale. As tears welled up in my eyes, she reached out to hold me. The moment was real, almost too real. Suddenly, we both pulled away, aware that our sympathetic embrace had turned sexual.

"I wish I were a physicist," I cried. "Maybe then I could understand time and maybe then I'd understand why all the months I spent with Siobhan are now just a flash, a blink of the eye."

"For me it's just the opposite," answered Margaret. "It feels like it's been a century since I've been home in med school, with Dylan. It's only been a couple of weeks." Her words struck a chord.

We must awaken from
all dreams,
no matter
how
glorious.
And then
reality comes
again.
Please let me
dream
once more.

The Indian Serenade
Percy Bysshe Shelley

I arise from dreams of thee
In the first sweet sleep of night,
When the winds are breathing low,
And the stars are shining bright:
I arise from dreams of thee,
And a spirit in my feet
Hath led me—who knows how?
To thy chamber window, Sweet!

The wandering airs they faint
On the dark, the silent stream—
The Champak odors fail
Like sweet thoughts in a dream;
The nightingale's complaint,
It dies upon her heart;—
As I must on thine,
Oh, belovèd as thou art!

Oh lift me from the grass!
I die! I faint! I fail!
Let they love in kisses rain
On my lips and eyelids pale.
My cheek is cold and white, alas!
My heart beats loud and fast;—
Oh! press it to thine own again,
Where it will break at last.

"That's the same few weeks that I've known you. But that's not the feeling I get. I can hardly remember not knowing you."

"Yes, but tomorrow I leave and we'll never see each other again. Patrick, time will pass until it's like it never happened at all, like we never met."

"I doubt that'll happen. But if it does then time is my enemy," I answered. A tense, almost unbearable silence followed, as we sat just apart, aware of every breath the other was taking. Margaret broke the silence and moved to me, gently touching her hand to my face. I took her hand and slowly kissed her palm.

"Did time just stop just then or did I imagine it?" she whispered. We kissed, slowly and effortlessly.

"It happened again, didn't it?" I answered in awe. "Maybe we can make time stop."

"Just for tonight," whispered Margaret.

I pulled Margaret close and we made love, with all the abandonment and tenderness of two people trying to capture a moment out of time, certain we would never see each other again.

Afterward, we held each other close and

"Maybe we can make time stop. Just for tonight."

". . . brown penny, brown penny
I am looped in the loops of her hair."

gazed out the window. I stood naked behind my
lady love, relishing the timeless moment, and
wrapped a lock of her hair around my hand.

"'I am looped in the loops of her hair,'" I
whispered.

"More poetry?"

"You just be glad I wasn't reciting poetry
when we were making love. I wasn't, was I?"

"No, you weren't. I was listening. I would
have known if you'd done that. What's it from?"

As I held you in my arms
for the first time,
these words came to
my mind. I knew
in that moment
that our destinies
were forever
intertwined.

Brown Penny
    W. B. Yeats

I whispered, 'I am too young,'
And then, 'I am old enough';
Wherefore I threw a penny
To find out if I might love.
'Go and love, go and love, young man,
If the lady be young and fair.'
Ah, penny, brown penny, brown penny,
I am looped in the loops of her hair.

O love is the crooked thing,
There is nobody wise enough
To find out all that is in it,
For he would be thinking of love
Till the stars had run away
And the shadows eaten the moon.
Ah, penny, brown penny, brown penny,
One cannot begin it too soon.

It was William Yeats's "Brown Penny," and I savored the words as I gently recited the verse to my angel.

The night was right as rain and just as magical. We made love again, and settled gently into sleep, entwined in each other's arms. When Margaret awoke the next morning, the reality of what had occurred the night before began to sink in. The stars were gone. The clocks had started ticking again.

I felt empowered, exhilarated by the night we'd shared together. But as she looked at the man sleeping peacefully beside her, Margaret must have felt bittersweet. Bewildered. Ashamed. Our week on Inishcrag had taken place somewhere out of time, and it had been wonderful. But Marty Saybrooke had a full life to return to back in Llanview. Med school. Internship. Residency. *And Dylan!* Despite their estrangement, he was deeply committed to her. Panic set in. What must have been going through her mind! How could she allow herself to become so involved with this charming Irishman? Was she in love with me—or was it simply the magic of Inishcrag and that blasted full moon?

I braced myself as Margaret broke the

An old Celtic fairy tale had brought us together under a full moon. But now it was morning. Where would we go from here?

news: She had to leave Inishcrag as soon as possible. Quickly, I gathered my swirling thoughts into a sentence.

"I may not fit in with your life's plans. So then, Margaret Saybrooke, throw away the plans," I implored. Margaret was further shaken back to reality by a telephone call from the United States. It was a man from her hometown, Llanview, Pennsylvania. His name was Todd Manning, and he was calling to inform Marty that a little girl, Paloma, whom she had befriended at Llanview Hospital, was dying of AIDS. The tot had only a short time to live, and her last wish was to see Marty again. There was no time to book a commercial flight, so Todd would take care of everything. Leaving his pregnant wife, Blair, behind in Llanview, Todd flew to Ireland to pick up Margaret and take her home to America.

As Margaret packed her bags for a hasty departure, I was nowhere to be found, for I'd been dragged back to the ruined Celtic church by Inspector Quilligan! Once there, he informed me of the real reason that the "Men of 21" were so desperate to recover the sheet music. It seemed that this nefarious terrorist group was plotting to assassinate someone—a

*Shakespeare and I do not always
share the same image of our
loves . . . yet we
love the same.*

Sonnet 130
William Shakespeare

My mistress' eyes are nothing like the sun;
Coral is far more red than her lips' red;
If snow be white, why then her breasts are dun;
If hairs be wires, black wires grow on her head.
I have seen roses damasked, red and white,
But no such roses see I in her cheeks,
And in some perfumes is there more delight
Than in the breath that from my mistress reeks.
I love to hear her speak, yet well I know
That music hath a far more pleasing sound.
I grant I never saw a goddess go;
My mistress when she walks treads on the ground.
And yet, by heaven, I think my love as rare,
As any she belied with false compare.

very, very big player—in the United States. They were using this piece of sheet music to pass a coded message that contained the information as to when and where the murder was to take place and who the victim was. With a sense of supreme urgency, Quilligan told me to "trust no one," not even a member of his own agency, the Special Branch. These were to be Quilligan's last words. A shot rang out and he fell to the ground, mortally wounded. I struggled to escape, but two men grabbed me.

I would discover later that Todd Manning arrived in Inishcrag to whisk Margaret back home to see little Paloma, but she did not want to leave—not without knowing that I was safe. Sensing a life-and-death situation, Todd promised that he would stay behind in Inishcrag and see that I—a man he'd never met—got off the island safely.

Before jetting home to Llanview, Margaret felt a strong need to come to terms with our relationship. She resolved to write a farewell note, but simply could not. Conflicted, she crumpled up the note—with its air of finality—and replaced it with a new one, which offered us a glimmer of hope. Margaret's note told me, "You were right. We can't end

Sonnet 24
William Shakespeare

Mine eye hath played the painter and hath stelled
Thy beauty's form in table of my heart;
My body is the frame wherein 'tis held,
And perspective it is best painter's art,
For through the painter must you see his skill
To find where your true image pictured lies,
Which in my bosom's shop is hanging still,
That hath his windows glazed with thine eyes.
Now see what good turns eyes for eyes have done:
Mine eyes have drawn thy shape, and thine for me
Are windows to my breast, wherethrough the sun
Delights to peep, to gaze therein on thee.
Yet eyes this cunning want to grace their art;
They draw but what they see, know not the heart.

this without knowing what it means. If you mean the things you said to me, then call me in Llanview."

My States-bound angel had come to Inishcrag looking for peace and strength, and found far more than she ever could have imagined. For both of us, nothing could ever live up to this magic time. But now, uncertain of what the future would bring, she was going home . . . to Dylan.

I managed to escape my captors and hurried back to the Wild Swan. Meeting up with the newly arrived American, Todd Manning, I was distressed to hear that Margaret had hurriedly departed. With two thugs on my tail, Todd devised a plan: He would create a diversion by donning my coat and walking out of the inn. Hopefully, the two pursuers would mistake him for me, giving me time to flee. Ingenious! But much too dangerous! I could not allow this innocent man to step head-first into such a precarious situation. And so I politely refused his offer to save my hide. However, this stubborn Yank refused to take no for an answer! Suddenly, he threw a well-aimed punch at my jaw, sending me, in dizzy desperation, to the floor! Then he snatched my coat

He Thinks of His Past Greatness When a Part of
    the Constellations of Heaven
        W. B. Yeats

I have drunk ale from the Country of the Young
And weep because I know all things now:
I have been a hazel-tree, and they hung
the Pilot Star and the Crooked Plough
Among my leaves in times out of mind:
I became a rush that horses tread:
I became a man, a hater of the wind,
Knowing one, out of all things, alone, that his head
May not lie on the breast nor his lips on the hair
Of the woman that he loves, until he dies.
O beast of the wilderness, bird of the air,
Must I endure your amorous cries?

How could I let her sail away into the night knowing I'd never see her again? Oh Lord, please keep Margaret Saybrooke safe from harm.

and fled out the door—only to be gunned down in a hail of bullets. The thugs pitched Todd's lifeless body into the trunk of their car. Later, they must have realized that they'd shot the wrong man, for they dumped the car over a cliff. Oh, what this blameless man had done for me! I couldn't help but wonder what he felt he owed Margaret. And with a pregnant new wife waiting Stateside! Obviously, Todd Manning must have felt a strong sense of obligation to

I'm forever indebted to Todd Manning for putting his life on the line to save my poor soul. The bastards shot him like a bloody dog because they thought he was me!

Margaret in order to so easily offer to risk his life for mine.

Grabbing Todd's passport, I headed for Dublin, determined to confront Chief Inspector Bass of the Irish Special Branch, but I stopped short of my goal when I stumbled upon the chilling information that Bass was one of the bad guys! A traitor, a member of the "Men of 21." Using Todd's passport, I boarded a plane for the United States. Destination: Llanview, Pennsylvania.

The news of Todd Manning's death sent shock waves through Llanview. His widow, Blair, was utterly devastated by the loss of the man she had married in a touching and beautiful ceremony just days earlier. Later, I would learn that Blair, blaming Marty Saybrooke for Todd's death, vowed to get revenge!

Margaret opened her door and stared in utter disbelief at the sight of my weary figure standing before her.

"Patrick! Thank God you're safe," she uttered, falling into my open arms. Our tender reunion was interrupted by the arrival of Margaret's other man, Dylan Moody. I hid, and listened to Dylan as he consoled Margaret (who blamed herself for Todd's death). This

After a perilous journey, I arrived in America — a stranger in a strange land. I felt little peace until my angel offered me a place to rest these weary bones. Ah, Margaret, the love we share is the only true thing I have ever known.

handsome, well-chiseled man seemed solid, secure, Margaret's rock. I could sense the strong feelings they shared. After he left, Margaret unwrapped some presents Mr. Kenneally had sent from Inishcrag, along with a newspaper bearing a headline that rocked Margaret's faith in me.

It read: "JILTED POET KILLS LOVER." I had been falsely accused of murdering Siobhan!

Despite my protestations, Margaret had every reason to doubt my sincerity, my honesty. How could she be anything less than terrified given the bloody typhoon of danger and death I'd brought to her life?

I go through life, unfeeling, dead, until I sleep and dream of you.

Sonnet 43
William Shakespeare

When most I wink, then do mine eyes best see,
For all the day they view things unrespected;
But when I sleep, in dreams they look on thee,
And, darkly bright, are bright in dark directed.
Then thou, whose shadow shadows doth make bright,
How would thy shadow's form form happy show
To the clear day with thy much clearer light,
When to unseeing eyes thy shade shines so!
How would, I say, mine eyes be blessèd made,
By looking on thee in the living day,
When in dead night thy fair imperfect shade
Through heavy sleep on sightless eyes doth stay!
All days are nights to see till I see thee,
All nights bright days when dreams do show thee me.

A phone call to Mr. Kenneally, the Irish innkeeper, further weakened Margaret's belief in me. Kenneally warned her not to trust me.

"The Dublin police have a witness who saw Patrick Thornhart shoot his girlfriend. The man is a cold-blooded killer." Margaret, devastated by her doubts, pounded me with questions: Was I a poet—or a ruthless killer? Her coldness stunned me. I tried to reassure her with a kiss, but Margaret, her head spinning, struggled free.

"Don't touch me," she screamed. Having no idea at the time that she had once been raped, I backed away, stunned by her rejection. Overcome with exhaustion, I pleaded with Margaret to let me stay and sleep for a few hours. Then, I promised, I would leave her alone forever. I settled into a restless sleep. Soon after I settled into my slumber, Margaret steeled herself , then picked up the phone, and placed a call to Llanview's District Attorney, Hank Gannon. *My angel was turning me in!*

I awoke to hear the tail end of her urgent call. Devastated by Margaret's change of heart, and unable to win her heart back—especially with the wail of sirens in the distance—I raced from her house, just seconds before I could be apprehended. Fleeing the scene, I could not

How Clear She Shines
Emily Brontë

How clear she shines! How quietly
I lie beneath her guardian light;
While heaven and earth are whispering me,
"To-morrow, wake, but dream to-night."

Yes, Fancy, come, my Fairy love!
These throbbing temples softly kiss;
And bend my lonely couch above
And bring me rest, and bring me bliss.

The world is going—Dark world, adieu!
Grim world, conceal thee till the day;
The heart, thou canst not all subdue,
Must still resist, if thou delay!

Thy love I will not, will not share;
Thy hatred only wakes a smile;
Thy griefs may wound—thy wrongs
   may tear,
But, oh, thy lies shall ne'er beguile!

While gazing on the stars that glow
Above me in that stormless sea
I long to hope that all the woe
Creation knows, is held in thee!

And this shall be my dream to-night—
I'll think the heaven of glorious spheres
Is rolling on its course of light
In endless bliss through endless years;

I'll think there's not one world above,
Far as these straining eyes can see,
Where Wisdom ever laughed at Love,
Or Virtue crouched to Infamy:

Where, writhing 'neath the strokes
   of Fate,
The mangled wretch was forced to smile;
To match his patience 'gainst her hate,
His heart rebellious all the while;

Where Pleasure still will lead to wrong,
And helpless Reason warn in vain;
And Truth is weak and Treachery strong,
And Joy the surest path to Pain;

And Peace, the lethargy of grief;
And Hope, a phantom of the soul;
And life, a labour void and brief;
And Death, the despot of the whole!

shake the image of Margaret turning her back on me. Time has tempered my initial feeling of disloyalty. Only now can I fathom the maelstrom of feelings that propelled her to pick up the telephone. My dear Margaret, rocked to the core by the conflicting fear and desire she felt for me! Feeling so fearful, so empty, so betrayed, Margaret turned to the one man she knew could offer her safety, stability, and trust—Dylan Moody!

Margaret's heart whispered "Patrick," but her head said "Dylan." Though haunted by memories of the poet who touched her soul in Inishcrag, Margaret accepted Dylan's proposal of marriage.

Waves of overwhelming hopelessness descended over me me upon learning the news of Margaret's engagement. This distressing news was compounded by the fact that Chief Inspector Bass had come to the United States—in search of his Irish fugitive! It was only then that I realized that I could not run forever. Utterly fatigued, and not wanting to jeopardize Margaret's safety, I turned myself over to the U.S. authorities.

Locked in the Llanview jail, I received an unexpected visitor. It was Margaret, more beau-

Longing
    Matthew Arnold

    Come to me in my dreams, and then
By day I shall be well again.
For then the night will more than pay
The hopeless longing of the day.

    Come, as thou cam'st a thousand times,
A messenger from radiant climes,
And smile on thy new world, and be
As kind to others as to me.

    Or, as thou never cam'st in sooth,
Come now, and let me dream it truth.
And part my hair, and kiss my brow,
And say—*My love! why sufferest thou?*

    Come to me in my dreams, and then
By day I shall be well again.
For then the night will more than pay
The hopeless longing of the day.

tiful than ever. Embittered by the incredible news of her engagement to Dylan, and yet still worried that Bass might hurt her, I made a painful decision. To keep Margaret safe, I must push her away. It would prove to be the most difficult task of my life.

"Go home, Margaret," I muttered. She stood her ground.

"Well, that's me—silver-tongued, brooding Irish poet. "Ah, penny, brown penny, brown penny, I am looped in the loops of her hair...'" Works...every time!

This sonnet reminds me of what I knew in my heart as I was forced to sit idly by, watching you deny the fire in your soul for the sake of duty.

Sonnet 116
William Shakespeare

Let me not to the marriage of true minds
Admit impediments; love is not love
Which alters when it alteration finds,
or bends with the remover to remove:
O no, it is an ever-fixèd mark
That looks on tempests and is never shaken;
It is the star to every wandering bark,
Whose worth's unknown, although his height be taken.
Love's not Time's fool, though rosy lips and cheeks
Within his bending sickle's compass come;
Love alters not with his brief hours and weeks,
But bears it out even to the edge of doom.
If this be error and upon me proved,
I never writ, nor no man ever loved.

"How about the truth? Finally, now, one last time, tell me the truth, Patrick. Did you kill Siobhan?"

"Isn't that what you read in the paper? Isn't that why you called the bloody police to come and get me?"

"I was scared!" she responded.

"Of *me*?"

"Yes. Scared and confused . . . I don't know. I don't know what to think. Everything I've heard and read since I left you in Inishcrag makes me think that I was wrong, that you killed Quilligan and Siobhan. Patrick, I trusted you enough to make love to you. Now either I made a horrendous mistake and I should never trust my feelings again, or you're an innocent man, caught in a very dangerous trap, please . . . I need to know." Quickly, I changed the subject.

"Are you really intending to marry this man, Dylan?" I asked, bracing for her answer.

"Yes."

"Do you love him, then?"

"Oh yes, I do."

"Well then, go away. Stay out of this," I interjected, trying to cover up the pain. "You want the truth? All right, I'll give you the truth. I needed help and you were there, and

It pained me so to lie to Margaret, to hurt her so deeply. But I know in my heart that it was for her own good, to keep her safely out of harm's way.

you were lost and so gullible and so convenient and I used you! And that's the truth."

Stung by my coldness, Margaret reached through the bars and tried to touch my hand. As I pulled away, she cried out.

"You said that the night we spent together changed your whole world!"

"Well, that's me—silver-tongued brooding Irish poet." I met her gaze, steely-eyed. Climbing onto the bench in my cell, I launched into a bitter recitation of the poem that shook our world. This time, my tone was bitter, caustic. "'Ah, penny, brown penny, brown penny, I am looped in the loops of her hair . . .' Works . . . every time!"

Margaret choked back a sob as she dashed away from my cell. With my parting words, I warned her not to tell anyone that she saw the sheet music "or you'll be in real trouble." Once she was out of sight, my resolve dissolved. Blinking back tears, I dropped to my knees, heartbroken, yet knowing that I had done my best to protect my angel from harm.

"I love you," I gasped, choking the words out. "I love you."

Chief Inspector Bass's continued presence in Llanview unnerved me. My traitorous coun-

Like fire and ice, each in our own way, keeps our love in our hearts.

My Love Is Like to Ice
Edmund Spenser

My love is like to ice, and I to fire:
How comes it then that this her cold so great
Is not dissolved through my so hot desire,
But harder grows the more I her entreat?
Or how comes it that my exceeding heat
Is not allayed by her heart-frozen cold,
But that I burn much more in boiling sweat,
And feel my flames augmented manifold?
What more miraculous thing may be told,
That fire, which all things melts, should harden ice,
And ice, which is congealed with senseless cold,
Should kindle fire by wonderful device?
Such is the power of love in gentle mind,
That it can alter all the course of kind.

tryman pressed Llanview's Police Commissioner Bo Buchanan to extradite me to Ireland. Alone with the commissioner, I urged Bo not to allow it!

"Chief Inspector Bass is a traitor and a killer. If you turn me over to him, you'll be turning me over to the very man who wants to kill me."

But who should Commissioner Buchanan believe—the ravings of a crazed, poetic refugee or the solemn words of a highly respected official of the Irish secret police? My instincts told me that Buchanan was a reasonable man, and I was correct. He solved his dilemma, at least temporarily, by stalling. By keeping me safely behind bars and refusing the extradition, Buchanan could carefully weigh all the evidence before making the decision to send me home. Still, locked in my dank cell, I grew impatient. I had to find a way to prove to the U.S. law enforcement authorities that Bass was an international terrorist! Stealing a St. Nick suit from a fellow inmate—a besotted, ersatz Santa Claus—I broke out of jail and headed for Bass's hotel room in search of any shred of evidence to support my claim. Once inside the room, I found just what I needed to link Bass

This simple poet can be quite resourceful when he needs to be! How does one escape from an American jail? Simple—just pinch a cloak from jolly ol' Saint Nick and let the reindeer whisk you away!

with the terrorists—a coin! It bore the telltale insignia: "21"

I filled Bo Buchanan in on my discovery as well as on everything I knew about the impending assassination plot. Fearing for Margaret's safety, I pleaded with the commissioner not to involve her in any aspect of the investigation.

Unbeknownst to me at the time, the widow Manning was incensed to learn of Margaret and Dylan's engagement. Blair blamed Margaret for her husband Todd's death, and in her mind, Marty Saybrooke had it all. With the power of her grief poured into hatred, Blair sprang into action. She had just the right resource to ruin Margaret—her own scandal-laden tabloid newspaper, the *Sun*. Immediately, she put Margaret's and my photographs on the front page, calling us "killers." Adding to the insult, she filed a "wrongful death" suit against us in the U.S. courts. There was no doubt about it—Mrs. Manning was out for blood!

Not content with the accounts of her husband Todd's death in Ireland, Blair went abroad to my native land to investigate further. At the Wild Swan Inn, she unearthed a secret that she could use to further her vicious vendetta.

All in All
Alfred Lord Tennyson

I am afraid the lie that we must live will kill the truth that is our love.

In Love, if Love be Love, if Love be ours,
Faith and unfaith can ne'er be equal powers:
Unfaith in aught is want of faith in all.

It is the little rift within the lute,
That by and by will make the music mute,
And ever widening slowly silence all.

The little rift within the lover's lute,
Or little pitted speck in garner'd fruit,
That rotting inward slowly molders all.

It is not worth the keeping: let it go:
But shall it? answer, darling, answer, no.
And trust me not at all or all in all.

Speaking with Mr. Kenneally, Blair learned that, while in Inishcrag, Margaret and I had shared a room. Back home in Llanview, Blair used the news to her advantage by goading Dylan Moody. Though I was not privy to their conversation, I can make a fair estimation of what transpired:

"I've heard that the lovebirds cuddled by the fire and went on long horseback rides." I'm sure she savored each word as it spewed forth, hitting its mark. Later, Dylan confronted Margaret.

"Did you share a room with Patrick Thornhart?" A shaken Margaret nervously evaded the question as she searched for the proper response. Dylan, barely containing his rage, asked it again. Margaret met his gaze.

"Yes," she answered, struggling to tell the truth and to avoid hurting her fiancé. Knowing Margaret as I do now, it must have been agonizing to engage in this painful confrontation. I know now that Dylan ran off, leaving Margaret anguished and guilt-ridden. Later, she would make a full confession, admitting that we had shared a night of passion in Ireland.

The engagement was *off!* A tormented

I would rather live one day experiencing love than a thousand never knowing what I feel for you.

O, Were I Loved as I Desire to Be!
Alfred Lord Tennyson

O, were I loved as I desire to be!
  What is there in the great sphere of the earth,
  Or range of evil between death and birth,
  That I should fear,—if I were loved by thee?
All the inner, all the outer world of pain,
  Clear love would pierce and cleave, if thou wert mine;
  As I have heard that somewhere in the main
  Fresh-water springs come up through bitter brine.
'T were joy, not fear, clasped hand in hand with thee,
  To wait for death—mute—careless of all ills,
  Apart upon a mountain, though the surge
Of some new deluge from a thousand hills
  Flung leagues of roaring foam into the gorge
  Below us, as far on as eye could see.

Margaret gave her dejected fiancé his engagement ring back. Had I known, I no doubt would have rejoiced to hear the news. However, at the time of my angel's dis-engagement, I was caught up in a plan to nail Chief Inspector Bass. And now, I had a formidable ally in my quest—Commissioner Bo Buchanan!

Bo, now convinced that there could be some truth to my claim that Chief Inspector Bass was somehow involved in an assassination plot orchestrated by the "Men of 21," took action. For protection, he took me far away—to a "safe house" in the mountains, owned by a kind and compassionate icon of Llanview life, Victoria Carpenter. Once there, Bo urged me to remember anything—any shred of information—that could help him prove that Bass was a turncoat terrorist. A bottle of Paddy's Irish Whiskey helped my thought processes. A few healthy swigs, and my memory improved vastly! Suddenly, I recalled an important clue: As Siobhan died in my arms, she uttered a single word, "Poseidon." *What could it mean?*

While I remained in the safe house, Bo returned to Llanview and shocked Margaret

Though life is torture without you,
I would never trade the miracle
of knowing you,
loving you . . .

Sonnet 29
William Shakespeare

When in disgrace with Fortune and men's eyes
I all alone beweep my outcast state,
And trouble deaf heaven with my bootless cries,
And look upon myself and curse my fate,
Wishing me like to one more rich in hope,
Featured like him, like him with friends possessed,
Desiring this man's art, and that man's scope,
With what I most enjoy contented least;
Yet, in these thoughts myself almost despising,
Haply I think on thee, and then my state,
Like to the lark at break of day arising
From sullen earth, sings hymns at heaven's gate;
For thy sweet love remembered such wealth brings
That then I scorn to change my state with kings.

with the news that he believed I was telling the truth.

"Innocent people are slated to die unless this plot can be stopped," Bo informed Margaret. "Won't you help?" I'm told she was less than cooperative, at least at first. According to Bo, she exploded, telling him that she could not offer her assistance.

"I've put Patrick Thornhart behind me! I've already lost my fiancé. I'm trying to keep my head above water in med school, and now you are asking me to go to a mountaintop for God knows how long with the man who put me in danger?" she cried.

Bo desperately needed Margaret's help to recall the missing notes to the song on the piece of sheet music. Margaret is a talented pianist, and she had seen and played the song on the piano in Ireland. Now he needed her assistance to reconstruct the missing portion of the song, knowing that once it was complete, the CIA would be able to break the code. Then, and only then, would the authorities know who the "Men of 21" planned to assassinate. It was possible, Bo claimed, that she was already being watched by Bass's people. So Bo pressed the issue, and convinced my head-

Sonnet 17
William Shakespeare

Who will believe my verse in times to come
If it were filled with your most high deserts?
Though yet, heaven knows, it is but as a tomb
Which hides your life and shows not half your parts.
If I could write the beauty of your eyes,
And in fresh numbers number all your graces,
The age to come would say 'This poet lies;
Such heavenly touches ne'er touched earthly faces.'
So should my papers, yellowed with their age,
Be scorned, like old men of less truth than tongue,
And your true rights be termed a poet's rage
And stretchèd metre of an antique song.
But were some child of yours alive that time,
You should live twice, in it and in my rhyme.

strong Margaret that she had no choice but to join our cause.

Later that afternoon, I flung open the cabin door, and gasped to find myself face to face with my angel. The sight of her made me both elated—and angry. I turned my fury . . . on Bo.

"What the bloody hell is she doing here? You were supposed to protect her," I howled. Bo urged us to put our differences aside and work to solve the mystery of the telltale music. With that, he walked out the door, leaving the two of us alone for the first time since I'd driven Margaret away with my words in our jail-house rendezvous. Immediately, our tiny cabin was thick with tension. With a distinct chill filling the air, Margaret and I worked to reconstruct the notes to the missing piece of sheet music. And in the process, we fondly recalled the memories of our Irish escapade. Slowly, the tension melted, only to be supplanted by *sexual* tension. Like old times, I shared with Margaret glorious tales of my youth in County Kildare, and enchanted her with breathless poetic recitations, such as a particular favorite of mine, "Romance," from the poet Robert Louis Stevenson.

It was just the two of us, in Viki's cabin, sharing stories about our childhoods, when I first recited this poem to Margaret. She was so achingly beautiful . . . and so sad. She felt wounded by me, as if I had betrayed her, when all I was trying to do was to protect her.

Romance
Robert Louis Stevenson

I will make you brooches and toys for your delight
Of birdsong at morning and star-shine at night.
I will make a palace fit for you and me
Of green days in forests and blue days at sea.

I will make my kitchen, and you shall keep your room
Where white flows the river and bright blows the broom.
And you shall wash your linen and keep your body white
In rainfall at morning and dewfall at night.

And this shall be for music when no one else is near,
The fine song for singing, the rare song to hear!
That only I remember, that only you admire,
Of the broad road that stretches and the roadside fire.

Lost in the moment, Margaret responded, allowing me to take her hand. Just as suddenly, she pulled back, growing more anxious as the confusion poured out of her.

"You keep reciting all these dreamy poems, and you keep spinning these little fairy tales. You've got to stop it. You want me to be this enchanted princess, but I'm not! I'm just Margaret Saybrooke, and that used to be enough until I let you pull me into your fantasy where nothing is real, it's just beautiful! Nothing is real! Where one minute you're telling me that you care about me and the next you're telling me you're just using me!"

"Can't you see what's real when you look into my eyes?" She averted my piercing eyes. "No, don't turn away. Look at me. I didn't use you, angel. I love you," I implored, pulling her close. I recall vividly how Margaret accepted my embrace, then again pulled away, frightened by her feelings!

"No, you're lying, you're lying," she cried out, the tears flowing freely.

"You know better than that, angel. I love you with all my heart, I have from the first day I saw you in the firelight on Inishcrag."

Still, she refused to allow herself to accept

The Silver Tassie
Robert Burns

Go fetch to me a pint o' wine
An' fill it in a silver tassie
That I may drink, before I go
A service [to my bonnie lassie].

my love. Not wanting to listen to what she called my "lies," Margaret grabbed her coat and raced blindly into the new-fallen snow. I was compelled to follow. Catching up to her, I made a heartfelt, last-ditch declaration of my love.

"I had to convince you . . . to keep you out of harm's way. You knew too much: names and places . . . and that bloody music. If Bass and his boys ever found out, I had to somehow push you away from me to protect you. Lot of good that did, huh? Look where you landed: here on this God-forsaken mountain with me. It's fate; I don't know. But I do know that I can't fight this any longer. And neither can you. It's time we both faced the truth." I pulled her into a passionate embrace. The fiercely passionate words continued to gush.

"You've got to believe me now when I tell you that the love we shared is the only true thing I have ever known. And all our best laid plans, and all our best intentions, they all came out to nothing. But here we are together because we're meant to be together."

"You'll say that today, but then tomorrow . . ." The hysteria rose in her voice, and she

You love me, with everything that is you. I can feel it, I can see it in your eyes. And if you deny that, you'll be doing the one thing you've trying so hard to avoid: you'll hurt Dylan, you'll hurt yourself, and God knows you'll kill me.

tried to get her footing in the deep snow. Calmly and persuasively, I interrupted her diatribe.

". . . and tomorrow, and tomorrow and the day after, and the day after that. I'm still going to protect you, Margaret, but I'm not going to do that by pushing you away. Can't you see there's nothing to keep us apart now? No secrets, no hidden agendas, no fiancés with engagement rings; it's just you and me. So you may as well just give up your fight and say it. Come on, Margaret, say that you love me." Tempted, she whispered her answer.

"I . . . can't."

"Yes, you can. SAY IT, " I encouraged. With renewed conviction, she repeated her answer.

"I can't. Don't you understand? I'm gonna marry Dylan! I have to!"

The words left me momentarily speechless. Margaret, struggling to catch her breath, tried to explain.

"When I met Dylan, I was lost. I was bitter. I was afraid to feel anything for anyone. He gave me back my life. He made me feel whole again."

My tone softened.

"What made you so bitter? What made

I've spent my share of lonely evenings
seeking solace in the bottom of a bottle.
Yet no amount of
Irish whiskey can
dull the pain of love.

A Drinking Song
W. B. Yeats

Wine comes in at the mouth
And love comes in at the eye;
That's all we know for truth
Before we grow old and die.
I lift the glass to my mouth,
I look at you, and I sigh.

you so sad? Please, Margaret, don't deny me the part of you that caused you so much pain. Help me understand."

Near collapse, Margaret's pain came to the surface as she explained to me, in quiet, deliberate words, why Dylan Moody was so important to her.

"You want to understand? I was raped, okay? Todd Manning raped me. Are you satisfied now?"

It was a closely guarded secret that she had not shared with me during our wonderful, revelatory days and nights in Inishcrag. I stood immobile in the snow as Margaret relived the horrible circumstances of the gang rape she had endured two years earlier. She explained to me about the paralyzing fear that she felt for months after the brutal attack by Todd and several of his fraternity brothers. And she revealed to me that it was Dylan who taught her how to feel again.

"And how do I repay him?" she cried in a wail of anguish and regret. "I have never hurt anyone like that . . . and I never will again. Especially Dylan because he deserves to be happy. So . . . I will marry him, and we will be happy. I WILL MARRY HIM, if he'll have me."

To Celia
Ben Jonson

Drink to me only with thine eyes,
    And I will pledge with mine;
Or leave a kiss but in the cup
    And I'll not look for wine.
The thirst that from the soul doth rise
    Doth ask a drink divine;
But might I of Jove's nectar sup,
    I would not change for thine.

I sent thee late a rosy wreath,
    Not so much honouring thee
As giving it a hope that there
    It could not withered be;
But thou thereon didst only breathe,
    And sent'st it back to me;
Since when it grows, and smells, I swear,
    Not of itself, but thee!

I was glad to have had this insightful exchange with the woman I loved so dearly. Our snowbound exchange gave me an ever-clearer window into Margaret's soul. I understood, for the first time, why Todd Manning felt such an urgent need to fulfill the commitment he made to Margaret in Inishcrag. I comprehended more than ever the terrible beauty so clearly evident in Miss Margaret Saybrooke. There had always seemed to be something so sad mixed in with all that beauty that made me wonder what had hurt her so much. She had told me of her parents' untimely passing, and the wrath inflicted upon her by her unloving aunt. But a rape! Oh, the pain she must have felt! Thank God she had someone. Thank God for Dylan. However, I now had a better understanding of why she stood by him. Margaret was not determined to marry Dylan Moody out of love. Obligation to this man was her true, though unrealized, motivation. I was her true love! I returned to Llanview energized, empowered, thinking that maybe not this minute, this hour, or even this day, but Margaret Saybrooke and I would be together!

Margaret returned home, only to receive Dylan's heartbreaking news that Paloma, the

She may have a penchant for vengeance, but Blair Manning has certainly proven her mettle to me. Raising a child on her own and running a thriving metropolitan newspaper — I admire a woman who's not afraid to take risks.

little girl with AIDS, had died. In a moment of shared grief, Dylan realized that his love for Margaret had never died. Once again, he asked her to marry him. Desperately craving the security I could not offer her, Margaret agreed to become Mrs. Dylan Moody.

The news left me disheartened once again, and it served to agitate Blair Manning even more. Strangely, she dropped her civil suit against Margaret and me, and I couldn't help but notice a distinct alteration in the way she dealt with me. Once she had been vitriolic and hateful upon encountering me. Now Blair Manning was forgiving—and sweet as Irish cream toward me! Obviously, the vengeful widow had changed her game plan, and I was somehow still involved. But how? What I did not know at the time was that Blair had decided that the most effective way to hurt Margaret was to seduce one of her two men— me! And that formidable task was made ever more facile in that I was now working in the Country Club stables, tending to her prize horse, Araby.

Margaret saw right through Blair's scheme and tried to warn me not to play into her hands.

The more I desire the dream of you, the more I live in hell.

Sonnet 129
William Shakespeare

Th'expense of spirit in a waste of shame
Is lust in action, and, till action, lust
Is perjured, murd'rous, bloody, full of blame,
Savage, extreme, rude, cruel, not to trust,
Enjoyed no sooner but despisèd straight,
Past reason hunted, and no sooner had,
Past reason hated as a swallowed bait,
On purpose laid to make the taker mad;
Mad in pursuit, and in possession so,
Had, having, and in quest to have, extreme,
A bliss in proof, and proved, a very woe,
Before, a joy proposed, behind, a dream.
All this the world well knows, yet none knows well
To shun the heaven that leads men to this hell.

"I know that it's none of my business what you do with your life, but when I saw you today with Blair I just felt like something bad was about to happen. I tried to shrug it off but I couldn't. She's setting us up, I can feel it."

"For what reason?" I inquired.

"To hurt you, to tear you apart if she could. Look, I've seen her, I know how she works. I just am not such an easy target."

"And I'm a sitting duck, right?" I shot back. "One question, Margaret, why do you care? So you came to warn me, but you don't care about me, is that right? Don't toy with me anymore, please."

Thanks to our successful work in the cabin, the American CIA cracked the secret code hidden in the notes of the song, and ascertained that the "Men of 21"—led by the mysterious Poseidon—planned to kill a key figure with a massive bomb. But who was the intended victim? Unbeknownst to the authorities, the assassination target was to be Bo's father, the oil tycoon Asa Buchanan! Disguised as Major Austin, a munitions expert, Bo Buchanan was able to infiltrate the terrorist organization. Lurking at the makeshift bomb factory where Bo was assembling a bomb for

Like our souls,
our dreams are one.

Daybreak
    Stephen Spender

At dawn she lay with her profile at that angle
Which, when she sleeps, seems the carved face of an angel.
Her hair a harp, the hand of a breeze follows
And plays, against the white cloud of the pillows.
Then, in a flush of rose, she woke, and her eyes that opened
Swam in blue through her rose flesh that dawned.
From her dew of lips, the drop of one word
Fell like the first of fountains: murmured
'Darling,' upon my ears the song of the first bird.
'My dream becomes my dream,' she said, 'come true.
I waken from you to my dream of you.'
Oh, my own wakened dream then dared assume
The audacity of her sleep. Our dreams
Poured into each other's arms, like streams.

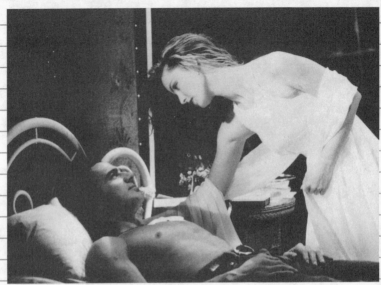

When a gunshot wound left me feverish and delirious, I surely would have perished had not Margaret nursed me back to health. I imagined in my half sleep that a peaceful angel had come to me in the silence of the night.

the "Men of 21" I overheard a conversation between Bass and the mysterious Poseidon and learned that they planned to double cross Major Austin (Bo). According to their heinous plan, the bomb Bo was constructing would explode as soon as Bo set the timer—killing him, as well as the intended target, instantly. Hearing this, I had to warn him! But before I could act, I was met by Bass, who pulled out a gun and shot me—point blank! The bullet left

I cannot love you more . . . then time, it seems, makes me a liar.

Sonnet 115
William Shakespeare

Those lines that I before have writ do lie,
Even those that said I could not love you dearer.
Yet then my judgement knew no reason why
My most full flame should afterwards burn clearer.
But reckoning Time, whose millioned accidents
Creep in 'twixt vows and change decrees of kings,
Tan sacred beauty, blunt the sharp'st intents,
Divert strong minds to th' course of alt'ring things—
Alas, why, fearing of Time's tyranny,
Might I not then say 'Now I love you best,'
When I was certain o'er incertainty,
Crowning the present, doubting of the rest?
Love is a babe; then might I not say so,
To give full growth to that which still doth grow

me critically wounded and delirious, but some-how I mustered up the strength to stagger to the one place I knew I could get assistance. I followed my instincts and reeled my way to Margaret's doorstep, then collapsed! My angel came to my aid, hiding me in her attic. However, my untimely arrival brought on a dilemma for Margaret: This was the eve of her marriage to Dylan, and in just a few hours the soon-to-be bride and groom would be attending their wedding rehearsal!

Feverish and shaking, I stared into my angel's eyes. Her heart obviously breaking, Margaret looked back. Like old times, I reached out and twined a strand of Margaret's silky hair around my quivering hand and whispered, "I am looped in the loops of your hair." How could I resist?

"Ah Margaret, you know you are breaking my heart," I sighed. Breaking the moment, she hurried off, visibly shaken by our close encounter. Though obviously overwhelmed with emotion on the eve of her marriage to another man, Margaret Saybrooke still could not admit to herself that she loved me! And I had never been any good at hiding my feelings. Alas, Margaret. Some part of her still hid in the

There is no one on this earth who knows Margaret Saybrooke as I do. No one who's loved her pilgrim soul and the sorrows of her changing face.

shadows, unable to face the truth we both felt in our bodies and in our souls.

With Margaret's marriage looming, I buried my pain and set out to save Bo, who I knew was in grave danger from the very bomb he was building for the "Men of 21." Using every ounce of my waning strength, I rose from my sickbed and hid in the trunk of Asa Buchanan's limousine, knowing that wherever Asa went, his son Bo would eventually turn up. Unbeknownst to me, Asa was headed for a deadly meeting with the "Men of 21" at the Palace Hotel—the very same place where Margaret and Dylan's rehearsal dinner was underway! I had to act fast to stop the bomb from detonating—or Margaret and her guests would die!

With time rapidly running out, Bo and I were captured by Bass and handcuffed to an overhead pipe. But a piece of cold, hard steel was not enough to stop us! We broke free and defused the bomb! The last ounce of my strength all but gone, I collapsed and was rushed to Llanview Hospital. To my immense satisfaction, Bass, that heinous traitor, was arrested.

I know in my heart that Margaret must

Like Mr. Burns's, my love will never die.

A Red, Red Rose
Robert Burns

O my luve's like a red, red rose,
  That's newly sprung in June;
O my luve's like the melodie
  That's sweetly play'd in tune.—

As fair art thou, my bonie lass,
  So deep in luve am I;
And I will luve thee still, my Dear,
  Till a' the seas gang dry.—

Till a' the seas gang dry, my Dear,
  And the rocks melt wi' the sun:
I will luve thee still, my Dear,
  While the sands o' life shall run.—

And fare thee weel, my only Luve!
  And far thee weel, a while!
And I will come again, my Luve,
  Tho' it were ten thousand mile!

have breathed a sigh of relief upon hearing that I would survive. Still, she was compelled to "do the right thing," and that meant marrying the man who offered her security and stability—Dylan.

On the day of the wedding, I was more determined than ever to see the woman I loved one last time. Although Blair tried to prevent me from leaving the stables, I hopped on her horse and galloped to the church. Finding

I galloped to the church, hoping beyond hope to persuade Margaret to abandon her foolish plans to marry Dylan Moody.

Many a poet has tried to express his deepest desire for the woman who has stolen his heart. But, Margaret, you are beyond the greatest poet's words. You render a prolific man speechless.

She Walks in Beauty
Lord Byron

She walks in beauty, like the night
  Of cloudless climes and starry skies;
And all that's best of dark and bright
  Meet in her aspect and her eyes:
Thus mellowed to that tender light
  Which heaven to gaudy day denies.

One shade the more, one ray the less,
  Had half impaired the nameless grace
Which waves in every raven tress,
  Or softly lightens o'er her face;
Where thoughts serenely sweet express
  How pure, how dear their dwelling place.

And on that cheek, and o'er that brow,
  So soft, so calm, yet eloquent,
The smiles that win, the tints that glow,
  But tell of days in goodness spent,
A mind at peace with all below,
  A heart whose love is innocent!

Margaret in the rectory, dressed in her wedding gown, I made a profoundly earnest appeal. The words came straight from my heart. They were my last hope.

"I want the same things you do, Margaret. A home, children, love that lasts a lifetime, peace. I want the passion that I know is in you. I want to free that wild heart that's inside you, somewhere deep inside you." Margaret urged me to stop, but I forged ahead with my last-ditch plea.

"There is a piece of land in the green hills of County Kildare with the stream as blue as the sky. And the nights so clear and so crisp you can almost touch them—touch the stars with your fingertips. I want to build our home there, with roses tangled rich over the red front door and a great big fireplace made with the stones cleared from our land—a home made from the very earth it stands on. And we'll be warm there in winter. And by the glow of the peat fire, I see you standing there, and you are holding our first child. She looks like you, God, she looks just like you. But she'll grow up loved like no other child. She'll not know the fear and loneliness you felt. She'll be free and fearless and loved as you are loved, Margaret—forever."

When the priest says, "Margaret, do you take this man to be your husband," and the time has come to answer, the Margaret I know, the woman I love, and I do, with all my heart— that woman won't be able to utter those words, not to any living man but me.

109

My angel stood in silence, seemingly paralyzed with pain. Sensing her weakened state, I challenged her again.

"When the priest says, "*Margaret, do you take this man to be your husband,*" and the time has come to answer, the Margaret I know, the woman I love, and I do, with all my heart—that woman won't be able to utter those words, not to any living man but me."

Had my fervent appeal hit its mark? Her face streaked with tears, an emotionally drained Margaret finally admitted to me that she had shared my deep feelings, but still, she had to be true to Dylan. She stuttered a bit as she uttered her final words.

"Goodbye . . . Patrick." Looking me straight in the eyes, Margaret slowly lowered the veil over her face, turned, and left the room. I watched in utter despair, tears streaming down my face.

Minutes later, a quiet murmur echoed through St. James Church as the wedding guests turned to see me standing at the back of the church.

"Do you take this man to be your husband?" asked Reverend Andrew Carpenter of Margaret. Resolutely and firmly, she looked at

Maybe not this minute, this hour, or even this day, but we will be together, Margaret and I heard her heart when I touched her on that never-to-be forgotten night when we made time stop.

Dylan and answered, "I do," adding the words, "with all my heart." Dylan smiled, reassured in her love. Surely my face showed the agony of my loss. I strode out of the church, running smack into the widow Manning! Pulling her up onto the horse, I dashed away to the stables. Once there, Blair played upon my anguish, luring me into an embrace. It felt wonderfully reassuring to be held so close—for an instant. However, a flood of memories of making tender love to Margaret washed over me. I broke free of Blair's grasp.

"Forget Margaret," she chastised. "She used you and walked away!"

"Shut your mouth or by God I'll shut it for you!" I roared back, still so tormented by the swirling events of the day. Yes, I still loved and wanted Margaret—but she was "Mrs. Moody" now. It was time to go home to Ireland.

I returned to my native land, but memories of Margaret Saybrooke filled my every thought. At Blair's urging, I returned to the U.S. and poured my energies into a new and exciting job: Professor of Western Literature at Llanview University. What a grand opportunity! What joy to be able to awaken a generation of young Americans to the power and

There's little doubt in my mind that Margaret made a most enchanting bride. Trouble is — she married the wrong man!

For just a moment, I tried to forget the seering pain I felt after watching Margaret marry another man— by allowing Mrs. Manning to offer me solace. Still, I found I could not run from what was in my heart, because running only makes the heart beat harder.

Should I have trusted Blair Manning? With seeming earnestness, she told me to "Forget Marty. She may love you, but she doesn't the guts to be with you. She never will." Were Blair's warning words keenly insightful or was she merely using me to get what she wanted?

beauty of poetry. A poem, you know, makes the imagination paint a picture inside your head. 'Tis a grand thing to do!

I thought it best to avoid the new Mrs. Moody. At the same time, I began squiring the widow Manning to events such as the first annual "Friends of Llanview" dinner, sponsored by Blair's newspaper, the *Sun*. The well-dressed

There is no pursuit more exciting than that of a woman who doesn't wish to be caught.

The Taming of the Shrew
Act 2, Scene 1
William Shakespeare

PETRUCCIO
Good morrow, Kate, for that's your name, I hear.
KATHARINA
Well have you heard, but something hard of hearing.
They call me Katharine that do talk of me.
PETRUCCIO
You lie, in faith, for you are called plain Kate,
And bonny Kate, and sometimes Kate the curst,
But Kate, the prettiest Kate in Christendom,
Kate of Kate Hall, my super-dainty Kate—
For dainties are all cates, and therefore 'Kate'—
Take this of me, Kate of my consolation:
Hearing thy mildness praised in every town,
Thy virtues spoke of, and thy beauty sounded—
Yet not so deeply as to thee belongs—
Myself am moved to woo thee for my wife.
KATHARINA
Moved? In good time. Let him that moved you hither
Re-move you hence. I knew you at the first
You were a movable.

PETRUCCIO

                Why, what's a movable?

KATHARINA

A joint-stool.

PETRUCCIO

          Thou hast hit it. Come, sit on me.

KATHARINA

Asses are made to bear, and so are you.

PETRUCCIO

Women are made to bear, and so are you.

KATHARINA

No such jade as you, if me you mean.

PETRUCCIO

Alas, good Kate, I will not burden thee,
For knowing thee to be but young and light.

KATHARINA

Too light for such a swain as you to catch,
And yet as heavy as my weight should be.

PETRUCCIO

Should be?—should buzz.

KATHARINA

               Well ta'en, and like a buzzard.

PETRUCCIO

O slow-winged turtle, shall a buzzard take thee?

KATHARINA
Ay, for a turtle, as he takes a buzzard.
PETRUCCIO
Come, come, you wasp, i'faith you are too angry.
KATHARINA
If I be waspish, best beware my sting.
PETRUCCIO
My remedy is then to pluck it out.
KATHARINA
Ay, if the fool could find it where it lies.
PETRUCCIO
Who knows not where a wasp does wear his sting?
In his tail.
KATHARINA
      In his tongue.
PETRUCCIO
                Whose tongue?
KATHARINA
Yours, if you talk of tales, and so farewell.
PETRUCCIO
What, with my tongue in your tail? Nay, come again,
Good Kate, I am a gentleman.
KATHARINA
              That I'll try.

She strikes him.

guests at this stylish function collectively gasped when the guest of honor turned out to be the notorious mobster Carlo Hesser, who had supposedly died three years earlier. As he stood before them in the flesh, it was obvious to all that Carlo was very much alive! The sight of the not-so-late mobster sent shock waves through the room, but it was Carlo's unmistakably deep and sultry voice that jolted me! I recognized it—as the voice of the Poseidon, the chief architect of the "Men of 21," whom I had overheard at the munitions factory on the day I was shot. Once again, this once-peaceful poet was drawn back into the spy game! I joined with Bo in an effort to prove that Carlo Hesser was not a reformed ex-mobster—he was now an international terrorist!

Despite her marriage to Dylan, fate continued to bring Margaret and me perilously close together. One night at the Llanview University library, we were both locked in past closing time. The chill between us momentarily melted when we read Shakespeare's *Romeo and Juliet* aloud to each other.

It was a special night, charged with unfulfilled sexual energy. The next morning, after our release, I was more convinced than ever

Any survey of Western literature must begin in the motherland of all great writing—Ireland, of course! And it must include the greatest playwright in Ireland, William O'Shakespeare. Oh, you were under the impression that Shakespeare was English? Well, never, ever, tell an Irishman that.

How foolish it seemed to find ourselves locked away from the rest of the world . . . letting ourselves, for a few brief moments, be 15 and in love for the first time. Still, it is a memory I cherish.

Romeo and Juliet
    Act 3, Scene 5
    William Shakespeare

        Enter Romeo and Juliet aloft [with the ladder of cords]

JULIET
    Wilt thou be gone? It is not yet near day.
    It was the nightingale, and not the lark,
    That pierced the fear-full hollow of thine ear.
    Nightly she sings on yon pom'granate tree.
    Believe me, love, it was the nightingale.

ROMEO
    It was the lark, the herald of the morn,
    No nightingale. Look, love, what envious streaks
    Do lace the severing clouds in yonder east.
    Night's candles are burnt out, and jocund day
    Stands tiptoe on the misty mountain tops.
    I must be gone and live, or stay and die.

JULIET
    Yon light is not daylight; I know it, I.
    It is some meteor that the sun exhaled
    To be to thee this night a torchbearer
    And light thee on thy way to Mantua.
    Therefore stay yet. Thou need'st not to be gone.

ROMEO

Let me be ta'en, let me be put to death.
I am content, so thou wilt have it so.
I'll say yon grey is not the morning's eye,
'Tis but the pale reflex of Cynthia's brow;
Nor that is not the lark whose notes do beat
The vaulty heaven so high above our heads.
How is't, my soul? Let's talk. It is not day.

JULIET

It is, it is. Hie hence, be gone, away.
It is the lark that sings so out of tune,
Straining harsh discords and unpleasing sharps.
Some say the lark makes sweet division;
This doth not so, for she divideth us.
O, now be gone! More light and light it grows.

ROMEO

More light and light, more dark and dark our woes.
Farewell, farewell! One kiss, and I'll descend.
     [He lets down the ladder of cords and goes down]

JULIET

Art thou gone so, love, lord, my husband, friend?
I must hear from thee every day in the hour,
For in a minute there are many days.
O, by this count I shall be much in years
Ere I again behold my Romeo.

that Margaret belonged to me! I went home to brood, and to Blair, who continued to try to manipulate me to her own ends. Margaret went home to Dylan—and faced his accusations. I later learned that he suspected—correctly—that I was still after her, but Margaret urged her husband to trust their wedding vows. Still, Dylan's agitation grew and nearly exploded one evening when we encountered each other in Angel Square. I was more than a bit inebriated, as my drinking partner Bo Buchanan can no doubt attest. As I poured the Paddy's down my throat, my lips loosened. And in times like these, it is only fitting to call upon the verses to sum up a man's feelings about the woman he loves—who happens to be married to another man.

Just as I spouted my pent-up disdain for Margaret and her marriage, who should walk into the square but the bride and groom themselves. Had it not been for the onlookers, my rival and I would have come to blows. Instead, we tempered our mutual anger and went our separate ways. Margaret went home—no doubt to diffuse her husband's fury by turning it into passion, while I vented my drink-induced fury in the square.

Locked away from the world, the icy chill between us momentarily thawed as we allowed the Bard's young star-crossed lovers to possess our souls. And when we touched, the whole universe was in our hands.

"I used to call her angel," I muttered, staring intently at the statue in the center of the square. With fierce accuracy, I hurled my bottle at the statue, and it made contact with a stinging crash.

That night of enraged expression proved to be an emotional catharsis for me. The simmering pot had finally boiled over, and it was time for change. For weeks after, Margaret and I made every effort to stay away from each other. Clearly, the situation was too explosive

I was well into my cups that night in Angel
Square when I began shouting this all-too-
knowing verse for all the world to hear.
I had no way of knowing
that you and your
devoted husband
were hearing
every word.

Lord Byron

Remember thee!   Remember thee!
    Till Lethe quench life's burning stream
Remorse and shame shall cling to thee,
    And haunt thee like a feverish dream!

Remember thee!   Ay, doubt it not.
    Thy husband too shall think of thee!
By neither shalt thou be forgot,
    Thou *false* to him, thou *fiend* to me!

for further encounters like the one that had occurred in Angel Square. Margaret threw her energies into her studies, while I, "Professor Thornhart," poured my heart into the most inspiring Western Lit classes that Llanview U. had ever seen! Secretly, I continued my quest to prove what I already knew—that Carlo Hesser was actually the evil Poseidon.

Discovering that Carlo was arranging a top-secret meeting aboard a yacht on the high seas, I rented a boat of my own and planned to follow—not realizing at the time that I was falling into Carlo's trap! Prior to my setting sail, Margaret happened to overhear Carlo Hesser on the telephone at Llanview Hospital. It would prove to be a fortuitous twist of fate.

"This is going to be turn into a mini-cele-bration," oozed Hesser. "The day Patrick Thornhart is out of our way forever!" Margaret listened to his every word!

Stunned and terrified by what she had just overheard, Margaret raced to the marina. The words spilled out in a great rush as she tried to stop me from heading out onto the high seas—and into Hesser's trap. Not wanting to involve her in this dangerous mission, I bitterly rejected her anguished plea.

Maybe Margaret does love Dylan., but she's in love with me!
Just as I am completely intoxicated by her.

"I bid you Godspeed, Margaret, back to your safe little home, and your safe little husband." My words stung Margaret, who fought back tears. Sensing her pain, I turned back, and with a finger, gently wiped away a tear from her cheek.

"I'd best be going," I offered tenderly. "But I thank you again for your concern—it means the world to me, truly. And it gives me a chance to say good-bye."

"You make it sound so *final*," she replied, fearfully. The possibility started sinking in on her—this good-bye could be the last. As I hurried away, Margaret was wild with apprehension, sensing I could die and we would never see each other again. Her face filled with sudden resolve—she wouldn't let it happen. She took a dramatic step. When I wasn't looking, she stowed away on my boat!

Sailing out to sea, I was unaware that Margaret was along for the ride, hidden under a tarp. When she finally revealed herself, I was furious! Now I would have to take her back to shore, losing track of Hesser in the process. However, before I could turn my ramshackle fishing boat around, the engine sputtered to a halt. Panic filled the foggy night air as we dis-

I both pity and envy my rival, Dylan Moody. He may have won
Margaret in body, but I have stolen her heart. If only she had the
courage of her convictions, she would with this poor poet be—and
not that barkeep she never should have married.

covered a hole in the boat. It was sinking! Hesser had sabotaged the vessel! The engine was dead, there was no radio, no phone, no life preservers, and no way out except to jump off the boat and swim. I forced myself to remain calm, acutely aware of Margaret's great fear of drowning.

"No! No! I can't do this!" she screamed. "This is how my parents died. Lost at sea . . ." I looked into her wild eyes.

"You were scared on Inishcrag, remember? But you came through—because you're strong, and ever so brave. Now, I need that Margaret back again—the Margaret I knew on Inishcrag. Come on, you're going to save yourself."

I hoped beyond hope that my inspirational exhortation would instill in Margaret a sense of strength she had never known before.

"Do you trust me?" I asked quietly.

"Yes."

"Then look at me. Don't look at the sea. Just look into my eyes. And we'll jump."

We took the fateful leap into the dark waters. Together.

Lit only by a faint sliver of the moon, Margaret and I clung tightly to a boat cushion,

Sailing out to sea in pursuit of Carlo Kesser, I was unaware that my dear Margaret was along for the ride, hiding under a tarp. I was furious—but only for a fleeting moment. How could I be angry with someone who cared enough to risk her life to be with me?

but the powerful ocean waves proved too much for Margaret, and she was knocked free. She went under, lost in the murky brine.

"Margaret!" I cried out, frantically reaching for her hand. "Oh God, don't take her from me now!" Precious seconds passed. At last, I caught a glimpse of her, coughing, disoriented, calling out my name over the sound of wind and waves. With one arm around the cushion, I reached out with my hand, calling to her to take it. Margaret desperately reached, first missing, and then finally grasping the cushion.

"I've got you!" I cried out in triumph. Meeting her frightened eyes, I willed my precious angel to survive.

"I'm with you, and we will make it to shore. I swear it!"

Hours passed, as we struggled to survive in the icy cold waters of the Atlantic. Only my arm, powerfully strong from shoeing horses in the stable, kept a weakened Margaret from sinking below the surface. To keep her spirits up, I wove tales of our exploits in Inishcrag. Just as despair began to squelch my forced optimism, I caught sight of a light in the distance. Land was at hand! With energy anew, I held Margaret close and valiantly made my way to shore.

"You were scared on Inishcrag, remember? But you came through—because you're strong, and ever so brave. Now, I need that Margaret back again—the Margaret I knew on Inishcrag. Come on, you're going to save yourself. Save yourself and jump!"

Elation instantly turned to fear when I noticed Margaret lying breathless in the sand. As I gently tried to shake some life into her, Margaret opened her eyes, barely seeing me. The frigid waters had taken their toll. Hypothermia had set in. Begging her not to die, I carried Margaret up the beach to a nearby fishing shack, where I warmed her under a blanket using the heat from my own body.

As the new day dawned, the enormity of the previous night's events began to wash over Margaret like the waves. Her mind wandered back to that horrifying moment at sea. She had already lost so much in her young life. Her parents. Her self-esteem. And, for a horrifying moment, me.

"I keep remembering you fading away into the fog . . . disappearing . . . the water so cold. And it keeps terrifying me every time. The thought of losing the man I love —"

Margaret stopped suddenly, the words having escaped before she could stop them. My eyes were fixed on her, frozen. I could not quite believe what I had heard. I took Margaret in my arms. She clung to me.

"Oh Margaret, don't you know by now? You will never lose me. Or my love."

Sonnet #18
    William Shakespeare

Shall I compare thee to a summer's day?
Thou art more lovely and more temperate:
Rough winds do shake the darling buds of May,
And summer's lease hath all too short a date:
Sometime too hot the eye of heaven shines,
And often is his gold complexion dimm'd;
And every fair from fair sometime declines,
By chance, or nature's changing course untrimm'd;
But thy eternal summer shall not fade,
Nor lose possession of that fair thou ow'st,
Nor shall death brag thou wander'st in his shade,
When in eternal lines to time thou grow'st,
So long as men can breathe, or eyes can see,
So long lives this, and this gives life to thee.

For hours, we talked, openly and freely, about our true feelings. Feelings that had been present ever since Inishcrag. Margaret came to understand that she had done what she'd always done.

"I ran from my feelings. Or I tried to," she finally acknowledged. As she spoke, I looked deep into her eyes as though trying to see through to her very soul. "Until last night, out there in the dark, knowing we might die . . . I couldn't deny it any longer. I can't lie to you or to myself. What you told me that day at Viki's cabin, what you've known all along—it's true, Patrick. I do love you."

Margaret's confession filled me with a contentment I had not felt since those days in which time stopped on the isle of Inishcrag.

"You wonder why I'm at peace?" I asked Margaret, kneeling down in front of her. "Don't you see? The world could end for me right now—and I'd have no regrets. Because I finally have the one thing I've always wanted—I have your love." My heartfelt words suddenly pained Margaret.

"Forever. And yet . . . because I love you . . . I can't feel that kind of peace," she told me, clearly still pondering her marriage to Dylan.

Credit: Donna Svennevik/ABC

I promise you—with all my heart—that our love is going to be a light. And it'll guide us thru the dark, and the sadness. All the way home.

Exacerbating her pain and guilt, Margaret had lost her wedding ring at sea. Over a dented tin cup of spearmint tea, I tenderly tried to help my fallen angel deal with her churning feelings. She never set out, I told her, to intentionally hurt Dylan. "I thought I could be free to love Dylan as much as he loved me. I tried," said Margaret. "But all I was doing was playing a part. I wanted to be the loving wife. But my heart still wanted you. Don't you see, if I'd listened to you in the first place—if I'd trusted your love—I wouldn't have done this terrible thing to Dylan."

I offered my own perspective.

"Maybe we have to make mistakes, Margaret, before we can hear what it is our hearts have always been trying to tell us. Yes, it is too late to undo the past. But we can learn from it. And it's not too late—for you and I to start building a life together."

Irresistibly drawn together, Margaret and I kissed with all the explosive force of our pent-up love and passion. I quietly cast Margaret under the spell of Yeats's "To an Isle in the Water."

"Our time will come, you'll see. We'll be together," I offered. Suffused with love, we sat

Margaret, you finally admitted what I'd known all along . . . that you loved me . . .

To an Isle in the Water
W. B. Yeats

Shy one, shy one,
Shy one of my heart,
She moves in the firelight
Pensively apart.

She carries in the dishes,
And lays them in a row.
To an isle in the water
With her would I go.

She carries in the candles,
And lights the curtained room,
Shy in the doorway
And shy in the gloom;

And shy as a rabbit,
Helpful and shy.
To an isle in the water
With her would I fly.

on the floor of the fishing shack, reunited at last, lost in each other's eyes. Suddenly, Dylan Moody appeared in the open doorway!

So intensely involved in each other, Margaret and I did not notice Dylan as he stood, taking in the scene. Suddenly, we both saw him. Mixed, swirling emotions filled the room. Shock—at Margaret seeing Dylan! Relief for Dylan—that Margaret was alive! Heartache—for me, as I watched Margaret jump up and fling her arms around her husband. But as she hugged Dylan, Margaret looked over his shoulder and exchanged a fraught look with me, sharing in my pain. As the reality of what he had stumbled upon sank in, Dylan peppered us with hard-hitting questions. Tempers flared. Margaret tried, but failed, to keep her two angry men apart.

"You and Marty spent the night *talking?* And I'm supposed to believe that?" asked an incredulous Dylan, the pitch of his voice rising with each word.

"What would you rather believe—that your wife is a tramp?" I countered, equally angry. The tension escalated to the breaking point. Dylan lunged at me, and Margaret tried to stop him. As he wrenched himself away from

Credit: Donna Svennevik/ABC

The world could end for me right now—and I'd have no regrets.
Because I finally have the one thing I've always wanted—
the heart of the woman I love.

her, Dylan abruptly fell, sharply striking his lower back.

"I'm fine, I'm fine," Dylan winced, refusing my helping hand as he staggered to his feet. "I just gave it a thump. I'll live."

Just then, a Coast Guard officer man stuck his head in the door, breaking the tension by informing our group it was time to shove off. We all walked warily out of the shack, the issue at hand still unresolved.

Tired and overwrought, Margaret returned home with Dylan and tried to postpone a confrontation. I knew in my heart that Margaret could no longer say the words she knew were no longer true. She could not tell Dylan that she loved him. However, gripped by fear, could she find the courage to tell him she needed to be free? I soon learned that her first attempt failed. She could not find the strength or the words to tell Dylan about our love.

I offered Margaret my life, my love, but the courage, I told her, "has to come from your heart." She insisted that the time had finally come—but privately I worried. Could Margaret do it?

Meeting in the Country Club stables, I gently told Margaret that I would be waiting for

*I have nothing . . .
only my heart to give to you.*

He Wishes for the Cloths of Heaven
W. B. Yeats

Had I the heavens' embroidered cloths,
Enwrought with golden and silver light,
The blue and the dim and the dark cloths
Of night and light and the half-light,
I would spread the cloths under your feet:
But I, being poor, have only my dreams;
I have spread my dreams under your feet;
Tread softly because you tread on my dreams.

her at the lookout on Llantano Mountain at sunset.

"If you don't come, then I'll know that is your answer." Taking a deep breath, Margaret assured me that, after telling Dylan the truth, she would meet me on the mountaintop. After one long last gaze into my hopeful Irish eyes, Margaret hurried off to finally have the telltale talk with her husband. Once Margaret was gone, Blair Manning stepped boldly out of the shadows.

"Don't hold your breath, Patrick," Blair chided. "Margaret will never have the guts to leave Dylan!" Despite her ominous prediction, I refused to listen, for I had faith in Margaret's love!

Margaret found Dylan taking out his rising frustration on the basketball court East Llanview's Community Center. She steeled herself for a confrontation. Catching sight of his wife, Dylan's anger escalated.

"Whatever you came here to say, just *say it!*" shouted Dylan as he continued to bounce the ball with ferocity. Margaret tried to get him to stop, but Dylan grew increasingly angry.

"Let's just get this over with. Are you leaving me or not?"

When I'm consumed by the dead still
air of regret, I think of you and
life is fresh again.

Sonnet 30
William Shakespeare

When to the sessions of sweet silent thought
I summon up remembrance of things past,
I sigh the lack of many a thing I sought,
And with old woes new wail my dear time's waste:
Then can I drown an eye, unused to flow,
For precious friends hid in death's dateless night,
And weep afresh love's long-since-cancell'd woe,
And moan th' expense of many a vanished sight:
Then can I grieve at grievances foregone,
And heavily from woe to woe tell o'er
The sad account of fore-bemoanèd moan,
White I new pay as if not paid before.
But if the while I think on thee, dear friend,
All losses are restored and sorrows end.

Dylan didn't wait for the answer to his indictment. Before Margaret could utter a response, he violently hurled the basketball away, letting out an involuntary cry of pain as he collapsed to the floor. It was Dylan's back—and the very same spot that he had injured in the fall in the island shack the previous day. Margaret accompanied Dylan, who was in great pain, to the hospital where the news was grim: He had chipped a bone and severely injured his spine. Dylan Moody required serious back surgery, and it would not be known for some time whether or not he would ever walk again. The news of Dylan's possible paralysis stunned Margaret. Tormented and ridden with guilt, she glanced at her watch and was stunned to see the time. She knew that I would be leaving at any minute for our fateful rendezvous on Llantano Mountain! Hoping to reach me in time, she quickly phoned the Country Club, asking the maître d' to deliver an urgent message to the stables.

"Please tell Mr. Thornhart that there been a medical emergency and I won't be able to come." However, the message would never reach me. It had been intercepted by someone

Despite how fate may shape our lives, remember . . . we did love once.

When You Are Old
W. B. Yeats

When you are old and grey and full of sleep,
And nodding by the fire, take down this book,
And slowly read, and dream of the soft look
Your eyes had once, and of their shadows deep;

How many loved your moments of glad grace,
And loved your beauty with love false or true,
But one man loved the pilgrim soul in you,
And loved the sorrows of your changing face;

And bending down beside the glowing bars,
Murmur, a little sadly, how Love fled
And paced upon the mountains overhead
And hid his face amid a crowd of stars.

else. If only I'd known at the time that the someone was *Blair!*

Full of love and hope, I peered out over the city from my mountaintop lookout, waiting my lady love's arrival.

"She'll come, I know she'll come. She's got to," I declared, nervously stroking the mane of the horse I had ridden up the mountain. As the hours passed, I grew ever more anxious. Finally, I heard a sound.

"Margaret!" I exclaimed, my voice slightly hoarse with relief and love. A shapely, feminine figure stepped out of the shadows. It wasn't Margaret at all. It was Blair! Pouring on her ever-seductive charm, she attempted to "console" me at my time of need. Despite Blair's insinuations, I refused to believe that Margaret had chosen to stay with Dylan. With fierce abandon, I mounted my stallion and galloped away, ignoring Blair's cries.

"Stop! Don't humiliate yourself!" she wailed to no avail. As the hoofbeats died away, Blair stood alone, foiled again.

I arrived at Margaret's house and stood petrified, stunned to see her doing a seemingly casual domestic chore. There she knelt, *picking posies!* I stared, rocked by the sight, as though

*If my thoughts were strong enough,
I could hold you in my arms . . .
instead, there's nothing here but tears.*

Sonnet 44
William Shakespeare

If the dull substance of my flesh were thought,
Injurious distance should not stop my way;
For then despite of space I would be brought,
From limits far remote, where thou dost stay.
No matter then although my foot did stand
Upon the farthest earth removed from thee;
For nimble thought can jump both sea and land
As soon as think the place where he would be.
But ah, thought kills me that I am not thought,
To leap large lengths of miles when thou art gone,
But that, so much of earth and water wrought,
I must attend time's leisure with my moan;
Receiving naught by elements so slow
But heavy tears, badges of either's woe.

the very ground were shifting under my feet. Then, feeling my face turning dark with anger, I whirled and disappeared.

Storming into the stables, I once again encountered Blair and let out my frustration.

"To see her standing there, like nothing was unusual, picking flowers, for God's sake! And me—waiting up there, like a bleedin' idiot. I can't believe it!" I seethed, firing a bottle against the stable wall.

"Patrick, please calm d—" interjected Blair, but like a headstrong Irishman is wont to do, I raged on, trashing the place. I sank to my knees. Truly moved, Blair put her arms around my fallen figure, hugging me silently. Unbeknownst to me, Margaret moved into the stables, stopping short at the shocking sight of this apparent betrayal. Seeing me in Blair's arms, Margaret hurried out. I never saw her, but something tells me that Blair witnessed Margaret's hasty retreat. A small, triumphant smile registered on her face.

"It'll be all right. I promise, Patrick, it'll be all right."

Dylan awoke from surgery, disoriented and panicked, with no feeling in his legs. He struggled to remember what had happened on the

Despite the sad truth that fills my days, I live in hope of one day loving you.

The Lark in the Clear Air
Samuel Ferguson

Dear thoughts are in my mind
And my soul soars enchanted,
As I hear the sweet lark sing
In the clear air of the day.
For a tender beaming smile
To my hope has been granted,
And tomorrow she shall hear
All my fond heart would say.

I shall tell her all my love,
All my soul's adoration;
And I think she will hear me
And will not say me nay.
It is this that fills my soul
With its joyous elation,
As I hear the sweet lark sing
In the clear air of the day.

*Dear Margaret . . . this is
my fondest wish.*

The Passionate Shepherd to His Love
Christopher Marlowe

Come live with me and be my love,
And we will all the pleasures prove
That hills and valleys, dales and fields,
Or woods or steepy mountain yields.

And we will sit upon the rocks,
And see the shepherds feed their flocks
By shallow rivers, to whose falls
Melodious birds sing madrigals.

And I will make thee beds of roses
And a thousand fragrant posies;
A cap of flowers, and a kirtle
Embroidered all with leaves of myrtle.

A gown made of the finest wool
Which from our pretty lambs we pull;
Fair-linèd slippers for the cold,
With buckles of the purest gold.

A belt of straw and ivy-buds
With coral clasps and amber studs:
And if these pleasures may thee move,
Come live with me and be my love.

The shepherd swains shall dance and sing
For thy delight each May morning:
If these delights thy mind may move,
Then live with me and be my love.

Her Reply
    Sir Walter Ralegh

If all the world and love were young,
And truth in every shepherd's tongue,
These pretty pleasures might me move
To live with thee and be thy love.

Time drives flocks from field to fold;
When rivers rage and rocks grow cold;
And Philomel becometh dumb;
The rest complains of cares to come.

The flowers do fade, and wanton fields
To wayward winter reckoning yields:
A honey tongue, a heart of gall,
Is fancy's spring, but sorrow's fall.

Thy gowns, thy shoes, thy beds of roses,
Thy cap, thy kirtle, and thy posies,
Soon break, soon wither—soon forgotten,
In folly ripe, in reason rotten.

Thy belt of straw and ivy-buds,
Thy coral clasps and amber studs,—
All these in me no means can move
To come to thee and be thy Love.

But could youth last, and love still breed,
Had joys no date, nor age no need,
Then these delights my mind might move
To live with thee and be thy Love.

basketball court, but the memories of his confrontation with Margaret were hazy. An agonizing decision faced Margaret: Should she stand by her husband while he dealt with the enormous challenge of walking again, or leave him, as planned, and start a new life with me? Only time would tell if Dylan would regain the use of his legs. Margaret understood that there was only so much medical science could do before the power of faith and love take over. Dylan's full recovery would depend as much on medicine as it would on his own determination and the support of his wife.

Days passed, and I occupied the anxious hours by concentrating on my classes at the university while waiting for Margaret to make up her mind about the future.

Then came the day I will not soon forget. In class, I was was winding down an impassioned lecture about Elizabeth Barrett Browning, reading one last sonnet, which so perfectly described the intensity and isolation of love, when all else drops away. Suddenly, as I finished reading the verse, a hush fell over the room as Margaret appeared.

The students filtered out of the classroom, leaving us alone in utter silence. Trying to read

No one can capture the intensity and pure emotion of love like Elizabeth Barrett Browning. These are for you.

How Do I Love Thee? Let Me Count the Ways
Elizabeth Barrett Browning

How do I love thee? Let me count the ways.
I love thee to the depth and breadth and height
My soul can reach, when feeling out of sight
For the ends of Being and ideal Grace.
I love thee to the level of everyday's
Most quiet need, by sun and candle-light.
I love thee freely, as men strive for Right;
I love thee purely, as they turn from Praise.
I love thee with the passion put to use
In my old griefs, and with my childhood's faith.
With my lost saints,—I love thee with the breath,
Smiles, tears, of all my life!—and, if God choose,
I shall but love thee better after death.

her expression, and seeing the pain in her face, I reached out to my angel. Filled with almost unbearable emotion, Margaret struggled to speak.

"Don't talk," I interrupted, sweeping her into my arms and an irresistible kiss. Rapidly regaining her senses, Margaret willed herself not to let time stop again. Holding back her pain, she broke the news that she was staying with her husband. I simply could not believe, nor accept, what I was being told.

"For God's sake, don't stay with the man out of pity," I bellowed, trying in desperation to reason with her. But Margaret remained strong and resolute.

"It's not about pity, Patrick. It's about honor, commitment, responsibility." She was doing what she had vowed to do.

My tone softened, and I gently informed her that I still loved her for her true and generous heart. Still, she mustn't forget that there was more to marriage than honor and commitment.

"It's about love. You love me, and God knows I love you!" I urged. Trembling, Margaret moved closer to me and, with great urgency, she stared into my eyes.

"If you love me, then there's one thing you

When Our Two Souls Stand Up Erect and Strong
Elizabeth Barrett Browning

When our two souls stand up erect and strong,
Face to face, silent, drawing nigh and nigher,
Until the lengthening wings break into fire
At either curved point,—what bitter wrong
Can the earth do to us, that we should not long
Be here contented? Think. In mounting higher,
The angels would press on us and aspire
To drop some golden orbs of perfect song
Into our deep, dear silence. Let us stay
Rather on earth, Beloved,—where the unfit
Contrarious moods of men recoil away
And isolate pure spirits, and permit
A place to stand and love in for a day,
With darkness and the death-hour rounding it.

must do for me. Let me go," she pleaded. Neither of us, she claimed, would have any chance of happiness, unless I agreed to set her free, thus freeing myself.

"There is no life without you," I responded, my voice filled with torment.

"There *has* to be," Margaret intensely whispered back. "And it begins right now."

With the last ounce of her strength, Margaret turned to leave, but I stopped her and, with renewed determination, reminded my dear one what it was like for me when she married Dylan.

I told her how I had pined for her, scorning her repeated requests to stay away because of the knowledge that was truly in her heart. Margaret listened to my heartfelt words, no doubt torn up inside. "I will not let that happen again," I somberly told her.

"Margaret, if you are telling me to go away, then that is what I will do. I will shut you out of my heart. So do not ask me to do this if you don't mean it. Search your heart—is this really what you want, Margaret?"

She took a deep breath. "Yes, it's what I want. I want you to have a life, a happy one, and not spend it regretting what never could

Leave memories behind and talk of love that's now.

XXXII
James Joyce

Rain has fallen all the day
O come among the laden trees.
The leaves lie thick upon the way
Of memories.

Staying a little by the way
Of memories shall we depart.
Come, my beloved, where I may
Speak to your heart.

have been." The words stung, and I fought to maintain my composure in the face of her certainty.

"So be it, then." I turned away, aimlessly fiddling with the books and papers on my desk, then looked up to see Margaret still standing there, unable to tear herself away.

"What are you still doing here?" I chided, the bitterness evident. "Go, just go."

Margaret hurried out the door, her resolve melting. I looked up at the empty doorway, and the impact of our parting suddenly sank in. Gripped by rage and despair, I could no longer contain my feelings. In one broad gesture, I swept my desk clean of all its papers and books. That was easy, effortless. But how, in Heaven's name, could I ever sweep the angel from my heart?

There is no one on this earth who knows Margaret Saybrooke
as I do. No one who's loved her pilgrim soul and the
sorrows of her changing face.

My dear Margaret. Will you ever realize how truly lovely
you are—in body and soul?. It's as if part of you
is always hiding in the shadows.

There is no time out of time. If there were, our love would have
stayed in a vacuum. It wouldn't have had any consequences.
It wouldn't have hurt anyone. But it has.

Poems of Love for Patrick

Patrick has shared some of his poems
and thoughts of love with you.

Do you have a special poem, one
that comes from your heart,
that you would like to share with Patrick?

Write it out and send it directly to him.
If you like, include your name
and address and send to:

PATRICK THORNHART
c/o ONE LIFE TO LIVE
77 WEST 66th STREET
NEW YORK, NY 10023